T0364155

The Invisible Library

THORVALD STEEN

The Invisible Library

✤

TRANSLATED BY JAMES ANDERSON

LONDON NEW YORK CALCUTTA

Seagull Books, 2018

First published in Norwegian as *Det usynlige biblioteket*
by Thorvald Steen

© Forlaget Oktober, Oslo, 2015

First published in English by Seagull Books, 2018

English translation © James Anderson, 2018

This translation has been published with the financial
support of NORLA

ISBN 978 0 8574 2 541 6

British Library Cataloguing-in-Publication Data
A catalogue record for this book is available from the British Library

Typeset by Seagull Books, Calcutta, India
Printed and bound by Maple Press, York, Pennsylvania, USA

CONTENTS

Antipater, Honoured Regent,
and our new ruler,

I am not to die tonight. I've been promised food if I write down all I know. I've agreed to this, provided it will be read to the king. Writing materials and an oil lamp are here before me on a small cedar-wood table. I'm housed in a room that's hardly more than two paces long and two wide. The walls are of white masonry. In one wall there is a hole through which I can see the entrance and the great parade ground of Nebuchadnezzar's palace. Here there's enough light for writing. I can make out the flat roof of the hall where the king is lying, paralysed from the neck down. Today was the first time I noticed the colourful animal decorations over the entrance: yellow elephants and ibises with golden beaks.

Priamos, the Macedonian king's cook, was hanged this morning, accused of poisoning King Alexander. I know that my superior was innocent.

I have a number of things to confess. When I finish writing them all down, you'll kill me.

A bunk has been brought in. It won't see much use. I'm sitting on a stool with a woollen blanket wrapped around me.

1

When the sun goes down it turns unbearably cold. I'll write until they come to fetch me. While I write, I live.

I was captured yesterday on the bank of the Euphrates, when the sun was at its height. The soldiers pushed me in front of them towards the palace, past the parade ground, to a room right next to where King Alexander is now lying.

There you sat, Antipater. Alexander's old friend and military mentor. You considered me for a while before you said to the soldiers standing behind me, 'From Aristotle's description, it can't be anyone but her.'

The soldier gripped my arm even tighter. When I was led past you, you grasped my hair and tugged.

'Haven't I seen you before?'

'Definitely not,' I lied.

'According to Aristotle as well as being the king's mistress, you also destroyed his mind.'

'Is that why I've been arrested?'

'Tell me what the king has been up to recently.'

You gazed at me with your large face. The few hairs still remaining to you, stuck out higgledy-piggledy.

'I've heard you can write.'

I nodded.

'My father was taught to read and write by a slave, I was there and I listened too.'

After a while you let go of my hair and gave orders for me to be brought here. My conditions aren't bad for a prisoner. I'm glad I'm not chained up in the dungeon.

Alexander lies in his great bed unable to move, while ever-more groups of people come to visit and observe him. Only eight days ago he and I shared a bed. I stroked his brow with my hand.

What I'm writing will cause Alexander to look for his sword, which he's unable to grasp. There he lies, soon to be a father, with the queen sitting by his side.

The king's friends and military leaders paid no more heed to me than if I'd been a small puff of wind, when I first became Alexander's mistress.

Now it's all over. Ten years of wars, against the Persians, the Babylonians, the Lydians, the Egyptians, the Indians and peoples I don't even know the names of, have been fought. Innumerable cites, of which Babylon, Samarkand and Tyre come immediately to mind, have been conquered. All the victories on the battlefield, all our trysts and all our love are past. Everything is lost.

The heat of the Mesopotamian flatlands had tormented us for days. For me, and nearly a hundred other cooks who accompanied the army, it got harder and harder to find food in the area south of Opis. The wheat and barley had shrivelled. The leeks, onions and lentils that we found were inedible. Helios played havoc with us. We, whose task it was to prepare food, were set to hunting birds and animals with bows and arrows and snares. We had to travel far from the camp to find food. The game had been scared away by the noise from the big tents.

The smiths and cartwrights repaired some of our vehicles before we continued eastward. We were heading across the Zagros Mountains in the Ionian highlands, towards Ecbatana in Media. More than five thousand soldiers rode in the vanguard. We followers numbered three thousand. Our army would conquer everything in its path, according to Alexander, and spread Greek civilization to the rest of the world. I assume the regent was living a more sedate life in Greece at this time?

It was boiling hot, we sweated inside the cart. One of its wheels had fallen off twice. At last we arrived at a great expanse of grassland, and the bumping ceased. I was sitting with a prostitute and her two children, four women who worked in the field kitchens, and two coopers. They'd been responsible for repairing the wheel. The leather awning protected us from the sun, but not the heat. Once the children had stopped crying, I dozed off. We were able to peer out through two large openings in the sides of the awning. I saw a few crooked willows by the side of the road. Between the trees a ribbon of milk-white mist had gathered. It turned a bit cooler. Corpses lay all around. Ravens, vultures and whatever other birds there were, circled above us. Vultures take the softest parts of the body first: the eyes, the nose, the open mouth. Man takes ornaments, coins and weapons. Decomposition does the rest, apart from the bones and the hair which lies in a wreath about the skull.

In the morning we rolled on through fertile Bisitun. Here were broad plains and fields of wheat and barley. Not far off I saw three stags and a flock of wild geese in front of a huddle of mud houses. The splendid landscape was opening up before us, bathed in ever-sharper light. A breeze swept the mist away, and the sharp contours of green expanses, brown plough land and shady orchards came into view. Hedges parcelled up the landscape before the distant powder-blue horizon. Here and there thorn bushes and thistles had been scorched by the sun, but the vast majority of things had been cultivated and watered, and were full of lushness. At last I could bake bread for the soldiers. They, like me, were famished.

After resting the night, we moved on. I sat in one of the carts right at the front. None of the officers who were riding at the head knew the way. We heard that the king was travelling by a faster route, which was impossible for carts.

Dusk fell. The first man we met, a shepherd with his sheep, was asked the way to Ecbatana. He shook his head. Our leader, an officer from Corinth, lifted the shepherd under his arms and laid him over his own horse, tore off his clothes and whipped him until the blood ran down his back, buttocks and thighs. Before he collapsed, he pointed the way.

It took the army an entire day to pass the dead shepherd. The thousands of soldiers left behind a broad fugue in the landscape.

My job was to feed fifty-four men. I'd made five pots of lamb, beans and fennel for them. Few in the tent knew what King Alexander looked like.

A soldier at the long wooden table stood up and announced that he supported the officers who deemed it pointless to pursue the rebels up into the mountains. Another soldier agreed and said that he hadn't been home in eight years. Few were surprised by that. Most of us had been away for more like ten. Several of them muttered, and then five soldiers shouted that the country was unfamiliar and dangerous. I hadn't finished dishing up the food. Anger simmered inside me. I put my ladle down and pushed my way over to the first man who'd spoken:

'Coward!'

The word sounded as if it had come from someone else's mouth. Everything went quiet.

'So you're quite happy that all our dead would have lost their lives for—'

I drew breath. '—nothing?', I shouted.

I'd never said anything in front of so many people before.

My husband had died some months ago by the River Indus. My parents were dead. I couldn't have supported myself if I'd been sent home to Pella. The army could provide me with work if it continued to conquer new territory. The army was my life.

Some of the soldiers began fighting.

'King Alexander's just a Persian whore!' one soldier shouted.

'He thinks he's a god. He's chucking our lives away!' yelled another.

I noticed a soldier in front of me chewing with quiet concentration. I hadn't seen him before. He swallowed the last of his meal, cleared his throat and rose.

The soldier turned to the two who'd just spoken.

'Deserters,' was the first word he uttered.

He was of medium height, had dusky skin and blonde, curly hair. He'd been silent until then. His powerful hands gripped the table top. He leant forward and looked around.

'I am your king,' he said without raising his voice, but loud enough for everyone to hear.

'Have you gone mad?' said the man sitting next to him.

'I am King Alexander, son of Philip II. My mother is Queen Olympias.

Several people shook their heads.

'It was I who, together with my father, subdued the Greek states. I am the ruler of Greece and Macedonia and the city states.'

Was he really our king? The one who'd founded his first city at the age of sixteen, and four years later took the throne after his father was assassinated? Was this the king who'd led the campaign against India?

His voice was high and rasping. Everyone stopped eating and turned. The men could have attacked the speaker and killed him. They were hardened soldiers.

'I've never seen him before, but I've heard that he's got a lopsided head,' one of the eldest men called out.

At that the murmuring ceased.

The speaker turned his gaze on me, picked up the last clean bowl, placed it directly in front of me on the table and said:

'Sit down, take my place, you're one of the few who deserve to eat. I shall serve you.'

I remained standing. He put his hands on my shoulders and pushed me down. I jumped up again. Was he making fun of me?

The battles with the Mallians, the awful march through the Gedrosian desert and the mutiny of his army here in Opis didn't seem to have left him with any visible scars. I knew he was thirty years old, like me, and the only man on earth who could conquer all races, and take every fortress and town.

There was a pounding in my temples. My mouth was dry.

'Sit down,' he repeated.

I obeyed.

He ladled the meat and beans into a bowl. I noticed that the men were staring at me.

He told me to eat, I swallowed three mouthfuls before I looked up at him again.

The men around us began to talk. Alexander raised his head. His face was deeply lined and powerful. It was the only time I ever saw him unshaven. His beard was blonde and bushy. He was muscular, a real athlete. His face had a somewhat ruddy tone. As did his neck and the area of chest that was visible above his tunic. His mouth was full, the lower lip protruding. A pouting mouth. His nose, on the other hand, was large and straight. His eyes were covered with a thin film of moisture, his gaze was intense and bright, it could have bored through iron. I noticed that he cocked his head somewhat to the left. Alexander later told me that he needed to do that to avoid seeing double. He said it was connected with a partial paralysis in his throat.

'You are beautiful,' he said, my hair falling across my shoulders as he removed the kerchief I wore on my head, 'I shall call you Penelope.'

I was about to say that my name was Phyllis, but I couldn't utter a sound. The men who were sitting closest, stood up and looked at us. He stroked my hair several times without saying anything, and then removed his hand, cleared his throat, took a deep breath and said in a loud, clear voice:

'Are all of you with me against the rebels?'

Everyone shouted yes.

'There was nothing in his clothes or appearance to make us want to follow him into battle and death. Our army numbered barely seven thousand incredibly exhausted men. As far as he was concerned there was no doubt about going on, it was something he never questioned. It was this self-assurance which not only allowed us to be led but also gave us strength.

My palms were moist. I tried to blink. I was staring right at him. I wanted to be his most devoted soldier.

He rose and walked calmly over to the first of the men who'd voiced their disgust.

'Get up!'

The man stood. Alexander's hand went to the hilt of his sword. The tall, thin soldier with his grey, unkempt beard, made no move to grasp his own. Alexander told the man to put his arms behind his back before he turned and pointed his sword at the three soldiers who'd so recently mocked him. One of them, the burliest, hesitated an instant, and then all three of them shoved the bearded man roughly in front of the king. Alexander stroked the blade of his sword lightly across the man's throat. Suddenly he lowered his arm, glanced at the men in the tent once more and said:

'I'm glad you wish to follow me.'

They fell to their knees. He ordered them to stand. Alexander nodded to his two accomplices, who came and stood by his side. They'd been testing the men's loyalty. The king drove his sword into the man in front of him. As he doubled up he was dragged from the tent, his blood turning the upper part of his tunic black. His mouth was open. The three who remained stood stock-still. Not one of the men begged for mercy, whined or pleaded. After all four had been taken away, the king ordered the soldiers to tend the horses and repair their swords and lances.

The soldiers loped away through the tent flap after they'd finished eating. I was still sitting on the bench. The king placed himself in front of me, ran his hand over my hair again and kissed my forehead. I glanced up. He had well-defined eyebrows.

'You saved me,' he said quietly, 'I won't ever forget that.'

He seemed a little awkward, and perhaps that was what gave me the courage to take his hand and squeeze it. I thought of all the men he'd killed with those powerful hands.

It won't be long now before I reveal how the king was poisoned. Alexander hasn't many days left to breathe. I don't know if, lying there, he entertains any thoughts about the sad fact that he, of all people, is to die in this manner.

It was so hot that first day I saw him. It was almost unbearable inside the tent. Beads of sweat ran from his hairline carrying the dust down his forehead, cheeks and chest. I noticed the scars on his neck and right hand. His forelock was plastered to his brow.

'Some days ago I told several thousand Greeks that I wanted to thank injured and elderly officers for their labours by sending them home and paying off their debts,' he said. 'It was meant as a kindness. You can't imagine what a scene it caused. The officers began stamping. They thought that the vanquished Persian officers were to be given their jobs in the army.'

I was both surprised and flattered that the king had turned to me, as a confidante. Or perhaps he had no one else to confide in?

'These are men who've fought for you for as much as ten years,' I said. 'No army has ever marched so far or fought so many battles. And they, with you, have won every single one. Maybe your Macedonian officers and soldiers thought they were about to lose everything, their privileges, and in some cases their fortunes?'

'I've been a fool,' Alexander said, 'I've spoilt them.'

'Why should we acknowledge, let alone respect, the gods of people we conquer?'

Alexander wasn't listening. He took out a kerchief and mopped the sweat from my face, before continuing:

'The ringleader, Lykistratos, was tall and blonde, green-eyed, a rather handsome, haughty Athenian. Would you believe that he got nearly a hundred officers to plan a mutiny?'

'Who and what are you referring to, my king?' I asked.

'I was afraid they might succeed. I had to demonstrate decisiveness and strength. I didn't permit Lykistratos to utter a single word in his defence. My three bodyguards stabbed him in the chest. I told them to place the corpse in a large bath of mortar. The body began to sink. Lykistratos had stiffened in a doubled-up posture. His eyes were open. His stomach and hips disappeared first. His head and feet stuck out. I put my hand on his brow and pushed his head under. The mortar covered his eyes, and Lykistratos sank. His head was completely submerged by the time the mortar set.'

Suddenly the tent flap was pulled aside. An officer appeared. His hair was black, his face reddish-brown with grey stubble. He was tall and bony.

'My king, your loyal soldiers await,' he shouted.

In a more subdued voice he added, 'They've been standing in line a good while.'

Alexander stroked my cheek.

'I must go now,' he said, and followed the officer with rapid steps.

I stood by the tent opening and looked out across the dry plain. In the distance the sun floated above the treetops. The grass was scorched and bent from the ravages of sun, hooves and boots. The king was almost a head shorter than his officer. A brown horse came towards them.

Alexander took the horse's reins. It lifted its head, swished its tail and kicked its hind legs. The horse straightened its neck, lowered its head, ready to butt, its mane fell forward, its back was arched with its tail in the air, it kicked again. Alexander tightened the reins, it seemed as if he was talking to the quadruped. He patted it for a long time, stroked its mane until it calmed down, then got into the saddle and spoke to the soldiers. It wasn't long before I could make out their cheers. The king leant forward as he rode around the men. Whether this was to talk or whisper to the horse, I've no idea.

Here follow a few illegible characters, possibly words or sentences. They're words, possibly sentences that have been lost. The language in the letter is Greek. There are crossings out. After that, some indistinct words before the statement, 'Nevertheless these words will eventually find their way into He biblietheke aoratos.' The term can be translated as The Invisible Library. *The text was written by a woman called Phyllis. It isn't dated, but was written in early June 323* BCE. *There are eight similar breaks in the text in various places.*

The king alluded to is Alexander of Macedonia, later known as Alexander the Great. The king's head cook was Priamos, and his responsibilities included ensuring that Alexander consumed no liquids or solids that might shorten his life. It's rare to find letters or texts containing narratives from women in Alexander's time. This is strange because the poet Sappho from Lesbos wrote three hundred years before Phyllis. Writers were usually male and came from the ruling classes.

The letter isn't formal, unlike so many examples from the same period. The literate had often learnt Homer, Herodotus and Thucydides by heart. The classics frequently permeated the style of the few who could read and write. It is possible that Phyllis' Macedonian background contributed to her unencumbered style.

Alexander is bedridden and paralysed from the neck down. Everything points to his having been poisoned. At school I learnt that Alexander was the greatest of all generals, that the places he conquered included Egypt, Persia and India, that his teacher was Aristotle and that he carried progress and our civilization eastward with him. I'd heard little about his final months. The letter dates from this period. Alexander has survived two attempted mutinies, combat fatigue has spread throughout his army. His idea of allowing conquered peoples to retain their own religions and languages is meeting with strong resistance among the king's Macedonian and Greek friends. Antipater and Aristotle are among the most prominent of these. They want the Greeks to rule the huge subjugated kingdom.

A few days before the letter is penned, Antipater has arrived from Greece and taken power. Aristotle has left Babylon. Antipater and his allies have no idea what Phyllis knows, as she begins to write.

We in the rearguard had unexpectedly found ourselves in the front line. I could see twisted bodies everywhere, greyish-white corpses and congealed blood, faces like black parchment, rain pouring down, bloody rags and shreds of flesh, wounded men on their knees begging for water, a dead horse with a gaping wound which revealed its entrails, and a young, dying man, his shining eyes rigidly fixed on some spot far away. Another, his face sickly yellow, painfully conscious of my stare, couldn't hide his terror. Shouted orders pierced the air above the stink of men and horses. Some had stood in mud up to their chests until the arrows liberated them, others lay wounded, unable to speak. A soldier tore the bandage from his neck, blood pumped out.

The enemy, we heard later, were the Cossaeans. They'd managed to divide our army so that only three or four thousand were in the vicinity. Our carts contained spears, bows and arrows. If the enemy launched a successful ambush, the army would have problems. In our train were all the king's carts loaded with much of the realm's valuables and his majesty's personal effects. If we were vanquished, Alexander's rule would be severely weakened.

A gaggle of women and children came walking towards us. The children were dirty and snotty-nosed. The cart halted in front of a rockslide. One of the women came right up to me and wanted to give me her baby, which she was carrying in a bundle. I looked her right in the eyes. I had the uncomfortable sensation that she resembled me. I spat at her. There is only one war: human being against human being. She dropped the baby on the ground, I looked away. As we moved on, I turned and just managed to glimpse the mother picking up her screaming child. We passed some mud huts, the stench was unendurable. A white-haired man was just managing to balance on a stool above the piss-sodden ground. Close by I could see a few plough furrows on a plot of land.

'They're like animals,' said the cooper, who was sitting in front of me.

More groups of fleeing people appeared. We drove them before us, they were like cattle. They looked as if they'd been rolled in mud. They were a people who needed conquering, it was the best thing for them. What a people! It wasn't soil they cultivated, but mire. In the future they'd become part of an advanced civilization. Ours.

We were deep in Cossaean territory. We lurched across grey fields. The drivers of our cart pushed open a heavy timber gate in a dried clay wall. Some flowerless plants clung to the wall, daubed with dirt. The carts were arranged in a circle on the ridge where we found ourselves, with a small conquered village close by. A couple of dead dogs lay near our cart.

In the village I saw a few children and an old man. He had dark skin and a pockmarked face, and was leading an emaciated camel which turned a creaking, dripping waterwheel. Five of our soldiers pushed the old man away, stabbed him with spears until he died and began to whip the camel until its hide was flayed. The terrified children ran off in all directions.

'Stop,' shouted an officer, 'don't you realize that the camel is the only thing that can get us water?'

The groaning wheel produced small squirts of water as wasps dived onto each drop that fell.

'Make the beast work,' shouted a spotty youth of a soldier, and let fly at the camel with a stick.

He didn't stop until the officer drew his sword and turned the point towards the stripling's throat.

When I got down from the cart, I caught sight of a pile of corpses in front of a hay barn. I took them to be Cossaeans. Next to it sat a black-haired boy with his head between his knees. The bodies lay in piles four high.

I had a quarter of a loaf in the canvas bag I carried on my back. I gave it to the boy, he threw it into the mud in front of him. I cuffed him.

Later in the morning our forces crushed the Cossaean army in a valley close by. Sixty-two of them fled in our direction. A scout had warned us. They must be tired and out of breath. We were behind our carts, waiting. We saw them between the oaks. They couldn't keep together. One of their men shouted. It sounded like an order. Four of them in a gaggle staggered up the slope.

'Get them,' shouted the officer behind me.

I sighted and let fly. Several arrows followed mine. Two of the men were hit and went down. The third ran zigzagging and shouting. He fell twice, but managed to scramble up and continued running towards us. Seven more Cossaeans appeared. They shouted. We couldn't understand what they were saying. By the time dusk came all the Cossaeans had fallen. Most of them breathed their last in the tall, dusty grass on the slope below me.

I can't hear anything outside. In here, in the little room where I'm a prisoner, my breath is the thing I listen to most. I try to tell myself that I'm reconciled to death and that I'm not scared of what will happen when I've finished writing.

I realize, Antipater, that you will use my letter in the power struggle after Alexander's demise. I'm no fool. The thought that somebody might ever release me, give me my freedom, send me back to Pella, draw a line under all I've done, and award me a pension for the rest of my life, is a hollow dream.

I wouldn't accept the offer. I would beg to remain undisturbed in my writing. I do not fear death. I do not fear silence.

When Father was away on campaign, my mother and I were often at loggerheads about how much work I should do inside the house and out. If I kept busy, my younger siblings would do more. Day after day she complained, 'None of you know how painful it is, waiting for your father, never knowing if he'll come home dead or alive.' Before I'd turned fifteen I had decided to marry a man I'd be together with all the time. Preferably an officer or at a pinch a soldier. I never wanted to stay at home waiting like her. I wanted to be where the army was. I despised my mother. 'You can do something with your fear, instead of nurturing it by passing it on to us children, the rest of the family and the neighbours,' I said. We didn't speak to each other for months after that.

On another occasion she said that if a king like Alexander could take his mother to his investiture, and not be embarrassed to be kissed by her, surely I could walk down the street with my mother without feeling ashamed? 'He's the king and rules the country, and you've never even managed to clean the mess you've made around the fireplace,' she said. 'These are the best years of your life, so just take things a little slower.'

When I think of my mother, I see her frail body, bowed down with work. She was always standing outside gazing across the stony scrap of ground which still promised countless years of grinding toil for her.

That same year I married Leandros; I was eighteen, he was twenty. I couldn't get away from home fast enough. He was the first man I'd ever seen naked. He was big and strong. He never hit me, the way my father hit my mother. Each time father came home from the front, there'd be a party at home, with presents, fish and meat, and lots of wine for the grown-ups. But after we children had been put to bed, I'd sometimes wake to hear Mother crying in the next room, with Father's sharp voice breaking in. Then there was silence, until I heard thuds on the wall.

I was convinced I'd never see Alexander again. A fortnight passed. All of a sudden he was standing there, a dark silhouette in the tent opening. We'd almost reached Ecbatana. There was a fluttering in my stomach and my throat felt dry. I was clearing away bowls and containers. He clasped my shoulder:

'Few things make me angrier than seeing my men mistreating horses.'

Why was he talking to me about horses? His voice had a tenderness which drew my attention.

'The horses are the ones that gallop in the front line when the enemy's army is bigger than ours. Horses see, horses think, horses have feelings. They're our finest soldiers.'

'My husband told me about Bucephalus,' I said.

Alexander ran his hand through his hair.

'That horse meant a lot to you,' I went on.

'Your eyes are so brown,' he said.

He drew breath.

'I asked first.'

'No death was harder to bear.'

'What about your father's?'

'No one was closer to me than Bucephalus. Philoneikes from Thessaly approached my father with a beautiful horse. He wanted thirteen talents for it, that's two years' pay for a general. I asked to see it. I was just a slip of a boy. Well, Penelope . . .' he said eagerly.

'Phyllis,' I said.

'What a sight it was: huge, brawny and black as coal, apart from its forehead. That was white. Its head was big and as broad as a bull's. "Bucephalus" was the first thing I uttered when I saw this magnificent horse. "Isn't Bull an odd name for a horse?" my father asked. "There's no other name for him," I replied. A powerful stallion's body with a bull's head. The king's own riders, four of them, tried to mount the wary horse and break it in. One after the other they were thrown. I glanced over at my father. He looked astonished. "They're not talking to him," I said. "They're playing havoc with him!" Father wasn't listening to me. "Take that crazy nag home with you," he yelled at Philoneikes, and turned away and kicked the ground. I shouted that he must listen to me. He pushed me away. His huge bodyguard tried to calm me. I shouted that I was his son. "He's our king, and yours too," the giant replied. I tore myself loose and ran over to the horse and Philoneikes, and asked him to let me have a try. Before Philoneikes could answer, I was holding the reins. As soon as I grasped them, alone with the animal, I was certain I could tame him, and I shouted, "By Zeus, I'll pay whatever the horse costs."'

Until then, Alexander's gaze had been lowered as he spoke, concentrating, as if he wanted to make sure that he told the story as accurately as possible. We were sitting on the benches by the tent wall. Now he smiled, the furrows in his brow smoothed out. He began to laugh. His laughter was loud and free, perhaps because it arrived so unexpectedly? He didn't laugh often.

I began thinking about how I'd had an early fondness for animals too, or insects to be more precise. I thought of my neighbours' bees back at home in Pella. Bees have just as many secrets as horses. I glanced at him and realized that it wasn't the moment to mention bees. He seemed absorbed in horses and in Bucephalus.

'The grown-ups laughed at me,' he said suddenly. 'I led Bucephalus away from the men and whispered to him before singing him a lullaby I'd learnt as a child, and walking in a wide circle around the men. After three circuits I led Bucephalus far away out of earshot. I stood him so that his head faced the sun. I did that so he wouldn't be able to see his own shadow. Only then did I look into his eyes. I was frightened it might be too soon. He let me stroke his muzzle for a long time, while I spoke of the weather and the landscape of mountains and wooded hills around Pella.'

Alexander raised his head.

'His eyes were as brown as yours. I climbed on his back and stroked his black mane.'

Alexander breathed deeply, shook his head and his eyes became moist.

'I've never felt my hands run through such a thick mane. I told Bucephalus that I wouldn't ride far, not that day, but that I wanted to ride him for ever, and that I'd never sat on such a high horse before, and that all the grass, straw, sand, earth and snow in the world was yearning for the tread of his hooves.'

'How did you break him in?' I asked.

'I held the reins taut, without tugging or jerking them, while I spoke to him and stroked his neck. Then I jumped down, walked calmly by his side, and every time Bucephalus turned his head to the left, I did the same, until finally he stopped altogether. He bent his great head, peered at me, let me lay my own head against his muzzle, before I mounted him again. I knew he was calm, and that I'd be able to control him with light touches of my heels and reins. I rode back to the men. My father smiled and shouted, "My boy, find a kingdom worthy of you. Macedonia isn't big enough."'

'Have you had any bad experiences with Bucephalus?' I enquired.

His face became grave. He spoke of a morning, two years before when he'd discovered that the horse wasn't grazing on the juicy meadow grass he'd been enjoying for a week. The army was ensconced in the mountains of the Mardians' kingdom. The Mardians had pulled back, but that night they'd managed to kill some of the king's bodyguards and remove Bucephalus to their headquarters. Five days later, two messengers arrived from the king of the Mardians. The messengers announced that their king was prepared to return Bucephalus if the army withdrew from their kingdom. Alexander thrust his sword into the dark-haired youth who'd conveyed the message. He told the other messenger that every woman and child in the Mardians' realm would be killed, and every house destroyed, one by one, if they didn't return Bucephalus immediately.

'Wouldn't you have done that for a friend, Phyllis?' he asked.

A few days later, fifty Mardians arrived at Alexander's tent. Bucephalus was being led by a slave who'd been sentenced to death. The Mardian soldiers felt certain that Alexander would kill the man who led the horse. But Alexander embraced each one of them, people he would have slain earlier in the day.

The leader of the contingent, a tall, wiry, grey-haired man with piercing, brown eyes, asked repeatedly if the king was satisfied with the gifts. Alexander told them to leave. He wanted to ride.

So far, Alexander had addressed me with great enthusiasm. Now he fell quiet. I wasn't sure if I was responsible for his silence.

'Have you ever been interested in bees?' I enquired.

He shook his head. I went on talking. He didn't stop me.

'In the springtime the beehives are taken to the plain outside Pella. It's important to have the hives in place before sunrise. There's nothing quite like spending the night next to them so that you can experience the first honey flight. As the sun rises, the bees fly out of the hives to seek the white flowers of the acacia tree. A boisterous, brown swarm of bees outlined against the red sky. A sweet dampness and the excited humming lingers in the air even after they're out of sight. Hundreds of thousands of them are off to their daily work.'

We stood up. Alexander's face was flushed, his eyes wide open. He was breathing heavily, he moved towards me, pulled off my tunic. I reached for his hand. He jerked it towards him. He shoved me towards the cask that stood right by us, bent me across it and pressed himself into me. I turned for an instant and saw Alexander's eyes, deep brown with tiny green points in the irises, before he pushed my head forward again. I felt his hands on my hips and met him by thrusting back. He lay down and told me to sit on top of him. When he came, his eyes became distant, his arms and hands released me. There was a special pleasure in watching the strength ebb from his body, as if for an instant I had power over him.

'Today hasn't turned out quite how I'd planned,' he said afterwards.

'I could do with a drink of water,' was all I could think of to say in reply.

Alexander was exhausted and needed sleep. He asked me to make sure he wasn't disturbed.

'But there's nothing to lie on here,' I said.

He pointed at the well-trodden earth floor, lay down and fell asleep instantly. I watched over his breathing, tried to follow his respiration. He was so peaceful and trusting. I touched his hair, I wanted to protect him during the coming night; a powerful, not very beautiful, sleeping man. I wanted the moment to last as long as possible, before once again we became cook and king.

Queen Roxane may come to hear about what I've written, when the letter is read to Alexander. That pleases me. If she feels Alexander's progeny kicking in her belly, won't she suffer a crippling fear? Surely she'll realize she has far too few friends to survive?

Do you know what I mean, Regent Antipater?

After I was widowed, I couldn't bear the thought of anyone touching my body. Two days after Leandros died, I was raped by three Greek officers. If I'd tried to resist they would have killed me.

'Why? I'm one of you,' was all I managed to say before they forced me to the ground and tore my clothes off.

'That's just it, we're fed up with those Persian tarts the king forces on us. We're want some Greek pussy,' Cassander said breathlessly.

The other two were Kyriostonides and Viliandros.

One of Leandros' subordinates, a soldier called Pyros, paid court to me a month later. He was a handsome man. As Pyros was proposing, I imagined the scornful remarks of Leandros' fellow officers about how I'd married beneath me, as if I'd committed some unpardonable offence. I said no and missed out on happiness with Pyros, because of narrow-minded people and my own cowardice.

Not long after, Pyros was killed by an arrow.

Each time the door is opened, it's as if the voices in the corridor get louder for a moment, before my ears get accustomed to the noise. I talk to myself aloud more and more often. Best of all would be a response from someone out there, to comfort me. If I do get a visit, the door will most likely be thrown open, and the soldiers will hurl me to the floor and press a blanket over my nose and mouth. As my strength wanes, they will press the blanket harder against my face. My flailing arms and legs will leave no traces. Not even a drop of blood, a graze or a bruise.

I fell asleep on the bunk, I dreamt of Leandros. We were following the army and the king. They were far ahead. We couldn't see them. We shouted. We didn't know where we were or where we were going. Dawn had begun to light up the landscape around us. My husband carried a spear in one hand and a sword in the other. There were steep mountains and barren sandstone hills in every direction. Wind and sun had conspired to weather them, the earth was white, as if it were covered with morning dew. Here and there deep ravines cut into the hillsides.

The only vegetation consisted of a few bushes whose thorny branches rasped in the wind. It raised the roofs of two deserted houses as if they'd been straw hats. The bare clay walls remained. The wind clawed at the landscape as we walked silently on. At the next fissure I wanted to leap down into the abyss.

The sky didn't turn blue. The horizon was bleached out. There was no rain there. The earth had been whipped so that nothing remained but loose stones of all shapes. Occasionally, a few clouds would appear, grey and black, as if to tease. They didn't bring a single drop. We didn't speak, we didn't cry, we didn't eat. The landscape ate us. My husband threw away his weapons, we clasped each other and heard the wind's teeth.

Seven years passed. Leandros survived one battle after the other. Forty-eight, if my maths is correct. In the end I thought that he couldn't die, that it was an impossibility. Countless times I've waited for weeks and months, inside our tent and out, thinking all hope was past, until suddenly he would be standing there in front of me. Exhausted, ragged, wounded and dirty, but alive. Only then could I breathe easily.

I lived in the tent with Leandros for much of the year: in towns, high up in the mountains or by the sea. It was a privilege a number of Macedonian officers and their wives enjoyed: being allowed to live together. I cooked the food and nursed him if he wasn't too badly injured. The only time he had to go to the field hospital was during the siege of Gaza, when he was hit by shot from a sling and lost the sight of his right eye. In the larger actions we could be separated for weeks. Then we followers would trail after the army in large carts hauled by donkeys, horses, camels and elephants. I would often help prepare meals for the soldiers. I wanted to be useful.

We reached the land the natives call India. I could hear the swell and the waves beating against the rocks on the shore. Leandros and I were convinced that we'd arrived at the sea, and that we'd be picked up by the fleet in the next few days and taken home. We'd arrived at the world's end, our task was over. Alexander had got the idea about the world's end from Aristotle. The king passed it on to his officers and soldiers.

Hundreds of us stood down by the water's edge. The water was warm. I had expected it to be green, blue or turquoise, but it was brown and not the least pretty. Everything ashore was of various shades of green, but dark green tints predominated. The leaves and plants were thicker than anything I'd seen before. The insects were large and the birds colourful. There were tall trees everywhere, and bushes and vegetation which seemed to be designed simply for filling up the small pockets of air between the branches of trees. We couldn't see a speck of sky. The forest was like a large, damp carpet which could have suffocated the entire army.

'This isn't a sea,' shouted one furious officer. 'This must be the River Indus.'

Some of us stood silent, others wept or wailed.

'See you at supper time,' was the last thing Leandros said to me. He and twenty other soldiers boarded a boat. They were to quell a small insurrection in the vicinity started by a couple of hundred natives.

That evening, just as I was about to go to bed, I heard a man calling my name. Kyrilos, one of Leandros' friends, was outside the tent. He told me that the boat had hardly put out from land before Leandros was struck by an arrow. Leandros had raised his arms in the air and shouted, 'Take care of Phyllis!' A strong current caught him up and dashed him against a rock, and then he disappeared in the torrents of water. Thirty-five soldiers had been hit by arrows before falling in the water. I would dearly love to have held his hand and drowned with him. For the next four nights a couple of officers' wives slept in my tent to prevent me throwing myself into the Indus.

My native city, Pella, was becoming depopulated, many of its inhabitants had died, but many more had gone as soldiers or officers to the army and were elsewhere in the world. I had nowhere to go. My parents were dead, I was twenty-eight. The pension Leandros left behind was too small to allow me to establish myself somewhere else. I had to continue following the army.

I've always enjoyed cooking. Making the fire, planning the meals and serving them to the men about to fight, and maybe die, for our country. A week after Leandros' death, I asked General Chrystomides for help. He knew Priamos, the king's chief cook. Priamos wouldn't employ me until he'd seen what I could do. Not far from Opis, before an open-air fire, he asked if I could roast a leg of mutton. 'Yes,' I replied. He disappeared behind the tent and came back with a sheep on a tether.

'There you are,' Priamos said handing me a long knife with a bloody handle.

The knife was heavier than I'd expected. I weighed it in my hand and asked Priamos to tighten the rope.

I plunged the knife into the animal's throat. As soon as the blade met some resistance, I forced it downwards, just as I'd seen my uncle do. The blood spurted out in an arc towards the ground. The sheep bleated once, shook its head, tried to butt me, its forelegs gave way, it fell on to its side, gurgling up blood, its tongue stuck out, and its head fell heavily on to the grass.

Priamos told me to dress the legs. He took the rest. When I'd finished, he said:

'I'll take you for two reasons: you were careful to wash all the blood off, and you waited until the fire had burnt down to embers before you began roasting. Far too many people singe the meat.'

I was allowed to keep the tent. Fortunately, the army needed cooks because so many of the kitchen staff had been lost in battle or to epidemics.

Being close to the soldiers' lives is what I love best. Hearing them talk of all the new peoples and animals they've seen, comforting them or rejoicing with them, it's quite different to being a cook at the palace.

The first task Priamos gave me in the kitchens here, was new to me. I was set to removing sea snails from their shells. The shells were as big as my hand. I thought I'd be cooking the snails in a dish. Priamos laughed. The people I was working with knew that these strange creatures were used to make a special indigo dye. Five cartloads piled high with snails were enough to dye one of Alexander's capes.

The first time Alexander and I ate alone here in his palace apartments, we sat opposite one another. For six months we'd had assignations on campaign, and for a month in the palace and the small Babylonian temple off the main street. We used to have sex and talk. On rare occasions, we shared an entire meal. It's something I shall miss. At such times, I had his full attention.

He ate so slowly. All the men I'd met ate quickly, Leandros was no exception. Alexander lifted his gaze from his plate, said a few words, smiled, gesticulated, cocked his head at even more of an angle, before fixing his eyes on the hare meat in front of him. Men eat as if they're frightened some predator will gobble up their food right in front of their eyes. Alexander listened, chewed, swallowed, then became distracted, as if he'd taken wing and flown off, before returning—to me.

That first evening alone in his apartments, he invited me into the innermost room. In the middle of the room was a table with a pot on it. He led me across to the table. A violet kerchief had been placed over the pot. He flicked it aside. I gasped and buried myself in him. He put his arms around me.

'It's a lobster. It's been boiled.'

'It's moving,' I shouted.

'Not for long. They're best when they're boiled alive.'

'But why is it red? I've heard they're black.'

'They turn red when they're boiled, isn't it pretty?'

He moved it across to a container of cold water next to the table. After a while he took it out again and placed it on a marble slab and smashed the shell with a stone. The meat inside was white.

'Open wide!'

I obeyed. The taste reminded me of salt water and the starry sky above it.

'How do you know so much about lobsters?'

'My teacher, Aristotle, asked me to send him lobsters a couple of years ago, and I didn't even know what they were. I had to send a messenger to Athens to enquire. As the army has advanced I've sent him skeletons, skulls, eggs and embryos of animals from plains, deserts, mountain chains and steppes. He can't get enough of them. He's explained in detail how I'm to note down everything I discover about these strange creatures we come across.'

'But surely, these are animals you and Aristotle have never seen before?'

'If the natives haven't got a name for them, I've sent suggestions which he occasionally adopts. I'm proud of that,' Alexander said colouring slightly. 'Aristotle has asked me to investigate the oddest things. I've kept some copies in my library.'

'What's the strangest thing he's asked you to do?'

'Find out how octopuses reproduce,' he replied.

'What is an octopus? Can I see your library?'

'Lysimachus is in charge of it.'

'Lysimachus?'

'A learned man Aristotle asked me to employ. You must have seen him, but he's hardly very memorable.'

'Perhaps living among words and dust is what he likes best?'

'The philosopher has taught me that the whale isn't a fish, it bears live young.'

'Hasn't he made you wise?'

'Aristotle says that all living things have their own status. Plants grow and reproduce. Animals can also move about freely. While human beings can make sensible decisions.'

'Are you saying that people are more sensible than Bucephalus or the bees?'

He made no answer.

'But where is the library?' I enquired eagerly.

'Next door.'

'Here in the palace?'

He pointed to a walnut-wood door just behind the curtain. It was small in comparison to the other doors, and completely undecorated. It looked like something he could have made himself, as if he hadn't wanted to involve others in what it concealed.

'Can we go in?'

'No,' said Alexander.

Roxane, like Admiral Nearchus, is dependent on Alexander's survival and ability to rule. Does Alexander believe that Roxane has entered into a pact with one or more of your military leaders to hand the throne to her unborn child after his death? That must be a lonely thought.

If there's one person Alexander could have done with here in Babylon, it's Olympias. The journey from Pella would have been a long one for her, but Alexander said she's in good health. She's the only one who was in a position to save him. But Olympias never came, and I didn't succeed either.

Antipater, both you and Aristotle have benefited from her absence. You've both had leisure to plot how the kingdom should be governed without Alexander. That statement isn't so very wide of the mark, is it?

It's barely three weeks since Alexander leant against the white door in its gold frame, leading to his main apartment. He looked like a painting, no, like a coin. I followed him in. He brushed the blonde lock away from his forehead with one hand. In the other he held a scroll; a messenger had come from his mother.

'What does she look like?' I asked.

'Olympias has never been beautiful, but she's certainly not ugly.'

'Are you fond of her?'

'She always seems to have so many things to juggle, holding the reins and trying to see what's happening behind her back the whole time. I admire her, but she's so suspicious. She's on the periphery of beauty, her hair is a bit too well combed, her make-up is a touch too heavily applied, she laughs readily and accompanies it with certain uneasy gestures that seem artificial. I haven't seen her for a long time. Some people find her so calculating that her company revolts them.'

'Do you feel that too?'

'She's my mother. If I die, her days will be numbered.'

Alexander's gaze began to wander. I knew what he was looking for. I'd placed the flagon of wine on the floor in the hope that he'd forget, or to be more accurate, postpone his drinking until the sun was at its zenith.

'Where have you hidden it?'

'You must have put it under the table by accident,' I lied.

He found it, took the cup from the table, drank, filled it three times, wiped his mouth with the sleeve of his tunic and asked:

'Should we attack Arabia?'

'The sooner the better,' I answered jokingly, 'we're going to pot here. But I know very little about Arabia.'

'You're clairvoyant, that's why I asked.'

'That's a slight exaggeration. I'm a grain of sand and you're a camel,' I replied.

He wasn't listening to me.

'This evening you can greet my brother,' he whispered.

'I didn't know he was in the city.'

'We shall watch his festival,' Alexander said. 'Some of my men have refurbished a small temple consecrated to Bel, the city god of Babylon. I bought it. It was too small for the believers in that part of the city.'

'What's this got to do with your brother?'

'Phyllis, you must allow me to keep my secret a little longer, and then you may have a wish.'

The temple had recently been whitewashed inside. A large bed, two white and gold vases, taller than Alexander, and a table with fruit and lofty, red flowers on it, was all that it contained.

'This is lovely, but where is your brother?'

'You can't see him. Dionysus is my brother. Dionysus is the son of Zeus, just as I am, and he's always with me.'

'Calling this a festival is a bit of an exaggeration, isn't it?'

'Undress!'

Quickly, he pulled off his gold-coloured tunic and fetched a box which he placed on the table. Inside were two flagons of wine and two masks.

I let my dress fall. He held out a mask.

'A dolphin, is that for me?'

'Naturally.'

He put on his own mask.

'And you're supposed to be a bee?'

Alexander nodded and smiled.

'I'm a drone, a creature that doesn't live long. But first . . . '

He got out two cups and filled them.

'I don't want much,' I said meekly.

'Don't insult my brother,' he said sternly.

For the rest of that evening and night we gratified Dionysus, and ourselves, until we fell asleep with our masks on.

I awoke to the sensation that something was touching my thighs. I raised my head and found myself staring at the largest bee I'd ever seen. He pushed the mask up on to his forehead and kissed me for a long time.

'What did you dream about?'

'About coins with my own head on them.'

'What are you going to do with them?'

'I'm going to take them to the shop and exchange them for something we can eat.'

'Are you hungry?' I asked amazed, because I knew it wasn't long since he'd been served a large meal.

'Ravenous,' he said laughing.

'You haven't forgotten that I'm allowed a wish?' I asked.

'I keep my promises.'

'You know how I've listened in to your conversations with the generals several times recently?'

'Get to the point.'

'The army seems exhausted.'

'What can you do about that, Phyllis?'

'I see you're rolling your eyes. Will you keep your word or not? I hope you're going to accept the offer of the Lydian and Carian army chiefs and let them take an active part with us in the campaign eastward, against the barbarians who are defending themselves so energetically. I'm afraid, Alexander. We in the army need all the help we can get, you know. We're encountering ever-stiffer resistance. Isn't that right?'

'Caria's army is hopeless.'

'Well, Lydia's army, then? You were the one who told me they'd sent you a combined message saying they 'could think of nothing nobler or more important than supporting you in the fight against the barbarians in the east".

'I don't know them well.'

'Our Greek and Macedonian soldiers are worn out after countless battles. Many haven't seen their homes in ten years. No army in history has been at war so long, conquered so much and marched so far. You are the only person who doesn't understand what I'm saying. Let the Lydian soldiers take part. I beg you. This in my only wish,' I said.

৯৫

I am male, Norwegian, and brought up to become a man. I've never owned a horse, I grew up in a winter sports' nation. My father taught me to move and jump on skis. My father's father taught his son the same thing. I was keen for my children to ski and jump. Alexander was a good rider. He was taught by his father.

Between the ages of seven and fourteen my father took me on long skiing trips at the end of each winter season. The trip got longer every year. As a seven-year-old I skied just under twenty miles. By the time I was fourteen, almost fifty miles. The hike was supposed to show how my strength, endurance and skiing abilities had developed from the previous year. The going was often heavy and the snow slushy at the end of March. We hadn't much food with us. Just like our polar explorers, when they reached the South and North Poles. Every year my ski jumps got bigger. I had two goals: to try the world's most important ski jump, Holmenkollen, and to enlist as a guardsman in the Royal Guards and learn how to do drill. Alexander got his horses to obey orders. My skis obeyed me.

It was 1967, I was thirteen and lived for ski jumping. When I wasn't training, sleeping, eating, going to school or listening to The Animals or The Doors' vocalist Jim Morrison, the perfect ski jump was my most vital concern. Interviewed that year, Morrison said he was reading Plutarch's description of Alexander's life, written almost eighteen hundred years earlier. Morrison grew his curly hair to resemble Alexander, and tilted his head to the side when he sang to imitate the king.

In 1970, the doctor forbade me to do any ski jumping because a genetic defect was causing a lack of protein production in the membranes of my muscle fibre. I began reading Plutarch to fill the void and to be like Jim Morrison. Over the next few months I was part of Alexander's army, close by him, a little behind, but never more than a horse's length away. As an adult I read Plutarch again:

'A painter puts a lot of work into the face of his model, especially the lines around the eyes, to render the inner likeness, everything else he places less emphasis on. In the same way, I must be allowed to dwell on the traits that expose the soul, and thus give a true picture of my people's lives.' From Plutarch to the present-day history is frequently promulgated as being the truth, as if the author has no agenda of his own.

Alexander is chained to his bed. The room envelopes him. I have a chronic disease which causes more and more of my muscles to become paralysed. My cell gets smaller every day. I don't give escape a single thought, for there is nowhere to flee to.

If I'd been someone else, the letter would never have reached me.

I won't get anything like fair treatment. Of course I won't. My archives are stored behind my forehead and eyes. What I'm writing will eventually end up in the Invisible Library. Historians won't write about Alexander's hands. It wasn't just that they were kind, loving and tender. They shone for me. I loved them, even the cracked skin. I couldn't imagine anything more beautiful, especially the fingers, with their frayed nails.

I've conquered fear before. Near the place where I grew up, lived a pair of wolves. My father and the other men of the neighbourhood tried to kill them on numerous occasions. The only traces the wolves left were sheep carcases. Once we found the remains of my uncle's dog. One ear was ripped off, and its belly and breast had been torn, exposing ribs and bones. Whenever my parents talked about wolves, they'd begin to stammer or sweat. They begged and exhorted us to be careful. We were three sisters. I was the eldest.

Mother was visiting her sick aunt a day's journey away. I was to take care of Agrippa and Larissa.

I'd just turned fourteen. Agrippa was eleven, but she only had the understanding of a four-year-old. Immediately after birth she was left out in the forest to die. An elderly man found her and knocked at my parents' door. The man was holding my sister in his arms when the door was opened. He asked mother and father if they knew who her parents were. They believed it was a sign from the gods telling them to allow Agrippa to live, and they took her back. She wasn't all that different from Alexander's brother, according to his description of him. Just like Arrhidaeus, Agrippa was terrified by the sight of naked flames. She only learnt to walk when she was five, and began talking, almost intelligibly, the year after. My youngest sister, Larissa, was five years my junior, and was playing with us down by the stream.

It was dusk. The heat of the recent spring days had hastened the snowmelt in the mountains, and the brooks and rivers were in spate. I'd promised my mother that we wouldn't wander further than the stream. 'Wolves won't cross the stream, they don't like water,' she told me. If we kept to our side of it, everything should be all right.

We were absorbed in our game, launching small boats of bark down the stream. Initially, Agrippa didn't understand when it was her turn, but after a bit of nudging and a good deal of patience from Larissa and me, we got her to understand the rules.

I knelt down. It was my turn to launch the boat. I was a short distance away from the others. Twice I'd mentioned that we ought to go back because it was getting dark. But twice I'd given in and agreed to sail the boat just once more. The noise of the stream prevented me from hearing the animal before it stood right in front of me. I told myself it couldn't be anything but a dog. I stared down at the grass and the moss, and then lifted my head warily and stole a quick glance at my sisters down the stream. I decided not to shout, it might frighten them and cause them to run off in different directions and become easier prey for the wolf. I dropped the bark boat into the water and let it drift. A large bush and a tree hid the beast and me from my sisters.

I brushed my hair out of my eyes. I'd never seen such a creature. Its coat was grey and wet, its eyes light blue. Its ears pointed straight up. I couldn't scream. I gasped. It shook itself. Mucus splattered my face. It raised one of its front paws. The stench of rotten meat came from its mouth. It took a pace forward. It opened its jaws. Its gums and front teeth were visible. I was sure that if those teeth bit me, it would be the last thing I'd know. I drew breath, I'd heard that you shouldn't look a wolf in the eyes. Silently, I prayed that the beast wouldn't go for my sisters. Why didn't it attack? The wolf shook its head. Was it standing like this trying to work out where to begin? I've never been so frightened, not even when the bodyguards obeyed Roxane's order to arrest me.

The wolf came a step nearer. My legs were paralysed, I couldn't run. As I bent down, it licked my brow quickly two or three times. I tried to raise my arms to protect myself. For a split second the eyes in the great, grey shaggy head looked almost timid. Larissa shouted at Agrippa. The wolf bit me hard on my right ankle. It only bit once. I clenched my jaws, my teeth grinding. Then it turned slowly and made off across the stream, the water up to its belly. After only a few paces it was swallowed up by the darkness and disappeared. I wiped away the blood with leaves and a kerchief I had around my neck. My sisters never noticed the wound once I'd put on the boots I'd left with them. With night came the pain. The wound healed, but something had been injured. That's why I limp. I couldn't tell my mother what had happened.

'What's become of Callisthenes?' Alexander asked at our last meeting.

'You're joking, aren't you? You mean your own historian?'

'You know quite well who I mean.'

'You killed him,' I said.

There can't have been many men Alexander admired more than Callisthenes. He wasn't just learned and beautiful, he was Aristotle's nephew. No one could match Callisthenes' description of the king and his army sailing across the Hellespont, 'how the prows cut sharp as sword blades through the waves', the battles with the Persians, the victory over Darius III and the march through Asia to Egypt and India. 'The sea parted for Alexander,' he wrote.

In every one of his battles, according to Callisthenes, most of Alexander's soldiers survived, whereas the enemy lost thousands upon thousands. Alexander conquered mountains, seas, peoples, cities and horizons, and the vanquished loved it, wrote Callisthenes.

When Alexander suffered a setback, Callisthenes would console the king and tell him that the gods wanted it that way because it was necessary for his future and ultimate triumph. The king would rule the world.

Callisthenes had served the king for seven years when Bactria was conquered. The army comprised officers from various subjugated peoples: Greeks, Egyptians, Persians and Indians. Alexander summoned the army top brass and ordered everyone, even his Macedonian and Greek officers, to salute him in the Persian manner; to kneel and kiss the king's hand, the proskynesis the Persians had performed in the presence of their king of kings since time immemorial. Would you have accepted it, Antipater? They were to defer to Alexander as if they were part of a conquered people. This they couldn't accept. When Alexander discovered your son throwing himself down in front of the nearest guard and kissing his hand, he grabbed him by the hair and banged his head on the marble floor until his whole face was covered in blood. The guards ran up and shouted to Alexander that Cassander was, after all, the son of his own regent.

I don't know what your son has told you, Antipater, but it was awful. Alexander seemed to be in a world of his own, according to Priamos, controlled by some invisible force. That was how your son came to have the scar over his left eye. All other versions are lies.

Alexander continued to bang his head on the floor until the guards overpowered the king and one of them said:

'Isn't it time for some wine?'

'Perhaps it is,' said Alexander.

He released Cassander and got to his feet. After a while he calmed down.

The following day Alexander organized a symposium. The theme was 'The principle of rapid movement during the battle of Issus'. Cassander wasn't in evidence. The servants brought out large quantities of undiluted wine. He introduced the philosopher Anaxarchus as if he were unknown. The king said that after Aristotle's death, he would be the most learned of all.

'What's this got to do with Issus?' Callisthenes asked, adjusting his tunic.

'Anaxarchus will introduce today's subject,' the king said, beckoning to the philosopher:

'Noble king, you will be worshipped as a god after your death.'

He stopped abruptly, before continuing in a shaky voice:

'So why should you not be called a god from now on, so you can enjoy it in mortal life?'

Alexander looked about, gauging the idea's reception.

At one time he'd been a real ruler, incensed by any fawning. Like the time, immediately after the battle of Hydaspes, when Aristobulus declaimed a poem to the king and his victory. In one of its stanzas he described how Alexander, with a thrust of his spear, had brought drown a huge elephant. Alexander tore the scroll out of his hands and threw it in the river. 'I ought to drown you as well,' he shouted.

At the symposium Alexander was quite a different man.

Callisthenes got up, coughed and said:

'Noble king, you are foremost among the brave, most regal among kings and best of all strategists, but I think it would be inauspicious to proclaim you as a god.'

'Why?' someone asked.

'It might perhaps disturb the intricate balance between gods and man, and arouse the anger of Olympus.'

Every face was turned towards Alexander. He filled his golden goblet with wine and handed it to the general standing nearest to him. The man drank and knelt. Then the king kissed him in the Persian manner, on both cheeks. And so the cup passed from officer to officer, until it came to Callisthenes. Callisthenes didn't genuflect. The king seemed not to notice but whispered some words to Hephaestion, his lover at the time. When Callisthenes went up to Alexander to receive his kiss, the king pushed his cheek away.

'Then I must live with one kiss less,' said Callisthenes.

Alexander didn't even grace him with a glance.

One of Hephaestion's messengers came running:

'Noble king, four of the young pages tried to murder you last night while you slept. They were armed with knives and swords.'

'Who trains the pages?' demanded Hephaestion.

'Callisthenes,' came the shout.

The king nodded.

The men around Alexander caught hold of Callisthenes and laid him on the floor. His feet were tied together and he was dragged into the dusty square outside. A cart, hauled by two horses, stood there.

Alexander was the last to emerge into the fine weather. Callisthenes began to scream. A kerchief was stuffed into his mouth and a cord tied firmly around his head so that he couldn't spit the cloth out. Three men climbed up on to the bed of the cart, and the horses began to move. They walked a few paces. They began to trot. The men in the cart drove the horses up and down the square. The onlookers cheered. Callisthenes twisted and thrashed his arms about at the cart's tail. His right arm fell off, then his left one. Only when his head loosened did the king go inside again and order more drink. The others followed.

Only a few days ago Alexander put his hands on my shoulders and gazed at me with mournful eyes:

'Why didn't you stop me then, Phyllis? I've got no chronicler now. Callisthenes is dead, and it's my fault. I read somewhere that there are five rules for being a good person. Sadly, I can't remember any of them.'

I smoothed his hair. 'You are irreplaceable, Alexander. There are plenty of scribes.'

'Thanks, I've become a little forgetful lately.'

We lay in bed, it was early morning in the palace. Alexander and ten of his best riders had agreed to practise some sword exercises. Exercises always took place early in the day. When we were first together, he never drank before leaving for such training. This morning he downed a flagon of undiluted wine. I asked if doing that wasn't dangerous. Alexander shoved me hard enough to knock me to the marble floor, and didn't apologize. Then he drank another flagon before getting dressed and going out.

I miss those first weeks and months we were together. On campaign it was easier to meet. Roxane was far away, in the nearest conquered city. Babylon was the beginning of the end for Alexander, and for the two of us. It wasn't just his drinking and the intrigues of the court, but his worsening health made it impossible for the army to advance. We were trapped and bogged down. We rotted in Babylon. I hate this city. I realized much too late that for weeks Babylon's outward splendour had distracted me from glimpsing our impending ruin.

One night, just before Aristotle came to the city, I recall Alexander waking and screaming that howling hyenas were trying to force their way in to get him. There was a solid mass of them in the doorway, like a furious, pulsating wedge of flesh, phlegm, froth and fur. Suddenly they worked themselves free, the king leapt out of bed and ran around the room with the animals snapping at his heels. I positioned myself in front of the window so that he wouldn't jump out. Twelve hours later he placed his feet on the floor, waddled over to the same window, opened it and peed, three storeys down, on to the parade ground. When I'd got him back to bed, he said:

'I dream about Antipater every night. Painful dreams, terrifying dreams. He hates me—and he has good reason to.'

'Sleep now,' I said and removed the flagon of wine from his bedside.

He clutched my arm and said:

'Are you worth any more than the other whores about the court?'

'So you assume I'm a whore?'

'If I hadn't protected you, you'd be dead,' Alexander said as he lay there naked and shining like pale gold.

'You're drunk,' I cut in.

The sight of him scared me. In the eyes of others I was doomed to be his dumb minion, less valued than a slave.

Through the hole in the wall I can see crows perched in the maples outside. All of a sudden they rise like black, living leaves, before clinging once more, each in his own place, to the bough. At dawn they fly off in great flocks towards the pale yellow streaks on the horizon.

I think about how many rooms separate Alexander and me in this palace. Several of them have been forgotten. They aren't visited for months. They get covered in cobwebs and vanish from our memories. Doors leading to rooms off back staircase landings can be neglected for so long that they heal over, become one with the wall which erases all trace of them, apart from a few chinks and cracks.

I've always envied Alexander's steadfast belief in the gods. I've tried, but now I'm tired of waiting for signs from them. I thought they'd help me when things got really bad. Do the gods actually care about me? Was I simply conceited and self-centred in believing that they would come to my aid when helplessness fills me? I was convinced that they would strike a light when darkness closes in, and lead me to clarity. That hasn't happened. The pain is stronger than the gods. Why don't they intercede? Aren't they interested in us human beings? Is it all a lie? An escape? Are we the ones that have conjured them in our heads? I have placed my life and my trust in the gods' hands. In vain. My loneliness has touched another's loneliness: his.

I shall miss lying in the grass looking up at the clouds, not to mention standing in the marketplace feeling a shaft of sunlight gently caressing my shoulder, in the crowd between the stalls of fish, grain, mushrooms, butchered hens and deer. I doubt I'll see scarabs in Hades. I don't mean the trinket I was given by Alexander, the one I wear around my neck and that symbolizes eternal life, no, I'm thinking about the beetle the jewel is supposed to represent. Those beautiful, metallic-looking beetles, green, yellow and mauve, consume the faeces of all other living creatures. The little insect spends all day shaping tiny balls of cowpat or horse dung, and rolling them to a suitable place to be eaten by the offspring she's expecting. I've heard that she carefully selects the most nutritious ones. As soon as the larvae emerge from their eggs, they eat one ball after another, until they grow plump and beautiful.

In war we become more brutal and cruel than normal. I've seen this in Alexander, Leandros, countless others and myself. But it's also true that after a few days of war we become friendlier, grateful that we are still alive. Hercules Demos, an officer who fought shoulder to shoulder with my husband for years, once told me when he was drunk that he used to beat his wife when he was at home. From the front he would write,

'Your Hercules, who kisses, caresses and hugs you each night, sends you his tenderest greetings.'

When Leandros died, I turned into a soldier without weapons, following the army until I became the soldiers' cook. In war, you're in the front line of life. There, you share what may be your last days and moments. Death is no more than an arrow or a sword thrust away. All at once, it seems that even the most brutish people want to pour their warmth and gentleness over their fellow soldiers. Men who have never paid homage to any god, start praying for dead or severely wounded comrades, a hymn to the fear that marks the face and constricts the throat. Soon Alexander will be the only one who doesn't understand: For the vast majority of the army survival is the most important thing. When the campaign started it was victory.

I grew up with the army. On the rare occasions father came home I loved examining his helmet, his thigh and chest armour, his lance and the short sword used for close combat, and trying them out. Whenever I let the sword touch my cheek, I felt a shiver of cold.

'It was my thigh armour that saved me from the Corinthians, Phyllis. Without it, their lances would have broken my legs, and then it wouldn't have been hard to drive a sword into me,' father said.

He brought his horse home with him once. It was fun. Mother was sceptical. Its name was Morning Sun and it was tethered to the gate outside. The chestnut stallion had a light mane. After everyone was asleep I crept out. The horse stamped nervously, whinnied and tossed its head. I was frightened, retreated a couple of steps, but then I began to talk to the horse about how scared I was that father would die on the battlefield, and how grateful I was that it brought him back safe to the lines every day. Finally, the horse allowed me to stroke it. I must have stood half the night running my hand over its head and back, while I pleaded that father must never be taken from us.

I was ten. I stared at Elias and at the yellow flames that flared beneath the sword blade. Father said he was the army's finest smith in Pella. Father explained that he was a Jew and believed in only one god. Elias had laughed and said that his god was superior to the god of smiths. I'd never seen Elias anywhere but in the smithy. I'm sure he'll be at his anvil still.

Visiting the army's joinery shop was nice, too. I caught the mild scent of pine from boards and planks, but nothing could compare with the smells of Elias' workplace; the acrid reek of sulphur which reminded me of the bits of lava father had picked up from Thera, the volcano on the island of Santorini.

It was dramatic and colourful at the smithy. The joinery shop was bright and smelt of forest, but there wasn't the same excitement.

'You need a clear flame,' Elias said.

He turned the blade with his tongs.

'First yellow heat, and then hotter.'

He had a pair of leather bellows with which he fanned the fire. The flames shot up.

'Not too quickly.'

Carefully, he removed the blade from the fire and laid it on the anvil, shimmering with heat and glowing yellow. He took his hammer which was leaning against the stone base of the anvil, and hammered away at the blade. The edge was hammered out on both sides before he put the blade back in the fire.

'We'll heat it up again, but a little less, until it's just red. The iron must stay in the fire just long enough to get to the right heat. Lots of people daydream on the job.'

The edge was orange, with bright, sparking nails. It was heated up for the second time, he gave it a few gentler blows.

'Lower heat gives the finest hardening, light cherry-coloured flames are what's needed. Water is best for cooling, with a little added salt to make it soft. Soft water makes the edge extra hard.'

The last time I saw Elias was when father told me to deliver a sword for sharpening. Elias told me a story I swore never to repeat.

'A few days ago King Philip and Prince Alexander were here,' he said. 'They had two servants with them. They told me to spread burning coals on the ground.'

He pointed past the anvil.

'What were the servants for?' I asked.

'They were ordered to leave, after showing the king the way here. I was told to make myself scarce, too, once I'd laid out a square of coals.'

'But why did they want it?'

'I was wondering that, too. I hid behind the shelter. As soon as they thought I was out of sight, the king and the prince removed their boots and, standing side by side, looked at one another, before staring at the coals which were still glowing. 'We are divine, my son. Your mother and I disagree about many things but that's one thing we're certain of,' said the king and held the prince's hand. Then they took two, maybe three rapid steps across the burning coals. Their screams were dreadful to hear.'

According to Elias they turned back, jumped clear, threw themselves on the grass and screamed for water for their scorched and bleeding feet.

'I ran after the servants who got hold of a cart and drove them home,' Elias explained. 'It's one thing to think you're a god, Phyllis, but just imagine if your mother and father do too—then you've really got a problem.'

Perhaps it's strange that, even when I hated Alexander most, I never told him that story. It wasn't really him but myself I was thinking about. I didn't relish seeing his reaction, which I assumed would be one of amazement. I had no desire to see him weak. I needed a protector, not a weakling.

My father, who was bigger, stronger and also more handsome than Alexander, belonged to King Philip's elite cavalry. I think they called themselves the Companion Cavalry, he was in charge of one of the eight elite squadrons of two hundred and twenty-five horsemen. He was disappointed when he wasn't chosen for the Royal Squadron. His pride in belonging to the military elite infected the whole family, especially me.

Philip inspected them once outside Pella. It was a big moment for the family to see father in his full uniform, before the army attacked Athens. I thought all royal personages were tall and good-looking. It surprised me that King Philip was a head shorter than my father and practically bald. His face was covered with scars, and he was blind in one eye. He wore a golden laurel wreath which had been presented to him by one of the generals. It was supposed to cover his injured eye, but the wreath made me stare incessantly at its golden leaves, behind which I thought I could glimpse the empty eye socket.

I lie on my bunk staring into the darkness. After a while it feels as if I'm somewhere beyond time.

The walls enfold me. The door in this small room is a closed mouth. My body isn't dead. It's waiting. I write, it's a compulsion, as if it can postpone death. When I lie full length on the bunk I can feel the pain in my ankle from the wolf's bite. When I sit down and write, I notice it less. This body is me. I breathe. It's something I do in order to write. Outside it's begun to rain, it makes no difference. The throbbing in my ankle reminds me that everything has its day.

The guards were shouting a while ago. I was frightened. When the heavy door opened, I looked straight into the face I've admired so many times for its symmetry, regular features and silky skin. Those brown eyes, brows, lashes, the straight nose, not too long, not too short, the three tiny freckles on the left cheek, the tall stature, the full lips, the long neck. I don't know how many times I've envied her, her looks, her make-up, her jewels and her elegant clothes. Alexander used to comfort me by saying that although the queen is a head taller than me, we have the same colour eyes and almost the same black hair, and in addition, unlike her, I can also read and write. Roxane stood before me, her belly swelling, painted, with glittering jewellery around her neck and arms. Her earrings were of amber and gold. She cast a quick glance in my direction and asked the guards why I had writing materials.

She took a step inside, looked about and pulled out a thin rope which she'd concealed beneath her dress. I hadn't time to get to my feet before she was standing next to me. Her perfume smelt of pine and apple.

'Stand up!' she shouted.

I stood in front of her.

She ran her hand rapidly over my stomach. She did it again. It was only then I realized she was making sure I wasn't pregnant. She placed the rope on the table:

'Please, do us a favour,' she said slowly, as if trying to make certain she was putting the words in the right order.

'There was a time when Alexander thought he could get around me by heaping me with jewellery—and he did. I seduced him at the victory banquet after he'd defeated my father, Oxyartes', army.'

'He raped you,' I said.

She pretended she hadn't heard. Her lips started trembling, she turned red, sweat broke out on her brow and she spoke a few disjointed words in Greek and Persian. I noticed that whenever she mentioned Alexander's name or mine, she spoke more rapidly and passionately. She began screaming at me.

One of the guards grasped her firmly by the shoulder.

'Use the rope,' she yelled on the way out.

I can't deny that the sense of having her in my power for the first time, gave me a moment of satisfaction.

Now I'm alone again. I can hear the occasional shouted order outside. Through the hole in the wall the scent of trees and flowers reaches me from outside. Summer is here.

Roxane is anxious, and with good reason, both for herself and for the child she's carrying. Unlike Alexander and me, she's got everything to lose. Alexander hasn't realized that over the past few months you, Regent Antipater, have manoeuvred yourself into the position of power you've been striving for in recent years. While the king spent his time drinking, you were plotting to become sole ruler of everything Alexander has conquered. Roxane is at the mercy of you and the army.

Alexander has never understood what Roxane's jealousy might unleash. He was misled into believing that because she'd put up with so much, she'd accept me.

I know that Roxane, and certainly Alexander's mother or Aristotle, would have had me put to death if they'd seen even the smallest bulge in my stomach. Perhaps some of those who were present that evening Alexander was poisoned would rather have a true Macedonian as heir to the throne? Roxane's child could never be anything but half-Persian.

I was pregnant once, eight years ago. I was taken ill not far from Gaugamela. I was eight months gone. Leandros got me into the field hospital late at night. I remember nothing more. Next morning I awoke amid moaning, wounded and dying soldiers. Leandros was nowhere to be seen. The stench was unbearable. I felt my stomach. It was slack. A man came running.

'Where's my husband?' I asked.

'He had to return to the battlefield to fight the . . .'

'Persians! Where's my baby?'

'He's behind the shelter.'

The thin man with his grey beard looked at me with calm, brown eyes.

'So it's a boy?' I said.

'He's lovely, he's lying in the hay.'

'Why?'

'So that he'll be comfortable.'

I was worn out, my legs and back ached. The only thought I had room for was that I wanted to lie down beside my child and shut my eyes.

'Do you know where I can sleep tonight?'

'On the grass outside.'

'Can you fetch my child? I'd like to hold him.'

'Are you serious?'

'Yes.'

'He's dead.'

'I only want to hold him for a minute.'

I must have dropped off. In a dream I saw Roxane's frightened eyes.

When she was here in the room, they were wild and desperate. She certainly fears for her life. I chucked the rope under the bunk.

It won't be long, Antipater, before your suspicions alight on her. Poor woman, her fall will be great. No doubt some people will remark on the similarity between Hephaestion's death and Alexander's present, albeit slower, decline after imbibing large quantities of wine. Strychnine and wine is an effective combination. The only difference is that Hephaestion died after a few hours. The amount of strychnine Alexander ingested was diluted with too much wine. Alexander's sufferings will last longer. It'll take days.

I saw Alexander and Hephaestion together two days before Hephaestion died. He was taller than Alexander, dark, muscular and with bright, green eyes. He really was beautiful. They were guests at the palace of Atropates, the satrap of Media, and were about to be driven by carriage to the stadium where competitions in discus, javelin and poetry reading were being held in honour of Dionysus. Three thousand artists from all over Greece had been invited. The servants announced that the public was already in place. I hid behind a crate and listened to them. I crept closer and looked at them through the slats. They were vying with each other to see who could balance the satrap's ceramic vases on his head for longest. The shouts, the laughter, the way they held one another, kissed and joked, left no room for doubt. I was jealous. A servant shouted that they must hurry and get to the stadium. Hephaestion laughed, dropped his vase on the marble floor and hummed.

You and all the other military leaders were indignant, weren't you, Antipater, when Alexander made Hephaestion a general against your will? It must have been convenient to have Hephaestion out of the way. Won't the knowledge that strychnine was used to poison him, and the fact that Alexander's body is full of the same poison, come to light one day? On the other hand: few can have forgotten just how intensely Roxane hated Hephaestion. What is your relationship to Roxane? Are you allies?

Alexander understands little of her language, and although she's learnt a few words of Greek, the silence at their meetings must be tedious. She is, and remains, a barbarian. Her appearance can't hide the fact.

Alexander's mother harped on for years about how he might be risking the entire kingdom unless he produced an heir. From being admired and coveted for her looks, the road to perdition is short for a queen who hasn't managed to rear a living prince.

Roxane knows that as far as she's concerned everything turns on whether it's a healthy boy. It's her only chance. How many times a day, I wonder, does she feel her belly to make certain there's life within? Is she hoping to give birth to someone who'll be close to her, someone she can confide in, someone she can talk to? The child will learn Greek at court. The conversations between mother and child will be halting at best. She must be one of the loneliest women in the world. I'm the one Alexander should have fathered a child with.

She's obsessed with her mountainous native country, her family, her language, the dances, the stories and the songs she grew up with. I can't understand why Alexander has never allowed Roxane to see her beloved Sogdiana again. It might perhaps have made life simpler and not driven her to be so hateful towards Alexander and me. Alexander never realized that she could be a greater threat than the Persian army and every other army put together.

Alexander has insisted we Macedonians accept the customs of the peoples we conquer. Nobody understands why we should follow rules that apply to inferior races. Not even Hephaestion. Priamos told me that when a delegation of Persian noblemen came on a visit, they fell on their knees before Alexander and bowed their heads. Hephaestion and several of the Companion Cavalry who were present, including one of Hephaestion's younger officers, said, in a voice loud enough for several people to hear, 'Go on. Bang your heads harder on the ground, the queen commands it.' Alexander grabbed the young man by the neck and shoved him so that he sprawled full length on the floor. 'There, you see,' he said, 'you're doing precisely what you were just laughing about.' The king's Macedonian friends blamed Roxane for introducing Persian customs at court. We're a proud people who have never bowed our heads to anyone. Alexander ought to realize that. Alexander, who's so famous for his courage, didn't defend her.

Any reasonably sensible man, and certainly a king, should have put more effort into getting the queen to learn Greek. Alexander hasn't provided her with a single teacher. The last time Nearchus came to dinner at the palace, she asked if she might be present. When the meal began, Alexander was surprised to see Roxane in the dining room.

'She's learning Greek by lip-reading,' Priamos answered, to lessen the queen's humiliation.

It wasn't long before the men overlooked her presence. Flagon after flagon of wine was placed on the table. She drank nothing. After a while none of them knew what Priamos and I were serving up. Nearchus rose, his outstretched arms grasping the table, fingers spread like fleshy starfish.

'Have you heard the one about Hephaestion's last visit to Glaucion the doctor?'

Alexander didn't get his answer in before the admiral began.

'He was worried he'd got a tumour on a gland just inside his arsehole. Hephaestion took all his clothes off. Glaucion told him to stand with his back to him, bend forward and spread his legs apart. The doctor took out a scroll describing the disease. Hephaestion looked over his shoulder at Glaucion and said, 'Shouldn't we do a bit of kissing first?''

Nearchus guffawed. Alexander struck him, got up and left. They hadn't noticed that Roxane had already fallen asleep and been carried out.

Although Alexander has told me many times that I'm beautiful, a thing most women like to hear, I've always known I could never match Roxane.

What would Alexander and Roxane talk about? They have no language in common, she's unable to share confidences. She knows nothing of Zeus, Odysseus or Cassandra, she's not acquainted with the stories he's immersed himself in so thoroughly. She's ignorant of the *Odyssey* and the *Iliad*. It's like not understanding day and night, hot and cold, west and east. Alexander should be the first to realize this.

Alexander fetched her from the furthest, loftiest mountains, the haunt of eagles, and lodged her in a succession of palaces in places he'd conquered. She was never where he felt most at home, among the soldiers. He's never known her.

Everyone who's written about Alexander concludes that he was intelligent. In spite of this, sources from antiquity to the present day point out that on the wedding night itself Alexander told Roxane, through an interpreter, that he was going to father a child

by his Persian first wife. These sources claim that he told his bride how gorgeous Barsine was. Roxane could well have reacted with grief and disappointment. Regardless of time, social status and language, can't such a reaction be understood? According to historians in our own age, Alexander wasn't merely intelligent, even if the episode from his wedding night tends to show otherwise but he also had a conscience and a soul. I would like to think that I know what a soul is too because I, in all likelihood, possess one. Although I'm fairly certain that it's not always functioning when I'm chopping onions or rinsing shaving water down the sink.

Alexander and I were, and are, literate people and have both experienced this strange condition of being somewhere on the road between life and death; where heartbeat, severance of the umbilical cord, respiration, hunger, digestion, arousal, loneliness, defecation, independence, detachment, hair loss and dust, punctuate our time on earth.

When Alexander and I looked up and tried to describe the clouds, we were always too late. In the blink of an eye they'd changed shape and sailed on towards new times and formations. We've never seen history or heard the grass grow.

I lie, I stretch out, food and air are forcing their way through my bowels. I can hear them. I have my hands on my stomach. I try to hum. I stop. My fingers have a special tranquillity. I hear birds outside. They glide, flap or rest with their feet on the ground or on branches. They're twittering about the wind.

I look at the stool I'm just about to sit on to write, to postpone my death.

There are screams outside my door. I rise. It sounds as if someone is being beaten and kicked. I can't make out if it's one person or several. It's horrible to listen to. I lay my head against the door. I keep my weight on my left foot. It relieves my painful ankle. I shout that no one has collected my slops bucket and that it smells disgusting, as if anyone cares. I look at my slender hands. I don't know why. I look over at the bunk. I sit, I write, letters I learnt as a child, Greek characters, living prints. My fingers obey my hand, my arm and my head.

Torture is a type of pain I won't be able to withstand. I'm scared I'll break down. I won't be able to hold on to my dignity, I'll turn into a helpless victim, ready to inform against anyone. Those are the limits of my bravery.

Antipater, you and the new rulers will see things in my letter which may be useful to you. They won't necessarily clash with what I want to write.

I look out, there isn't a soul there, not a bird singing. It's dusk. All rectangles: ceiling, walls, floor, bunk, door, turn into vague stripes, before they are erased and finally, as now, are no more than a memory in the darkness, a perception of stripes and rectangles. The only thing I can hear is my own swallowing and breathing. Gulps and breath, that's me. The thought that I'm sitting here alone and that darkness has consumed all the rectangles, causes my throat to swallow harder and my lungs to take in air more and more rapidly.

Alexander brought an amphora of wine. He placed it behind the bed with two silver goblets. His intimates at court thought he'd gone to the temple to pray. He poured for us both, drank his off and poured again. I ran my hand through his hair, put my cheek against his and said:

'Do you realize that Roxane told Priamos I was to be eliminated? She says it was your direct order. Priamos told her that he only takes instructions directly from you.'

'I don't know anything about this.'

'Roxane is jealous and dangerous. She's capable of making common cause with many of the Macedonian and Greek army men in your inner circle, who hate you!'

'Are you clairvoyant?'

'Certainly not,' I answered irritably.

'You just being modest. You're a modern-day Cassandra!'

'If you think I'll take that as a compliment, you're wrong. Cassandra was deeply unhappy about being able to see into the future. If you take a child that can't swim and drop it into the sea, saying it's going to drown hardly makes you clairvoyant.'

'Phyllis, you're just being modest, d'you hear?'

'Go on with you! How many times do I have to listen to that stupid story of Homer's about Cassandra, Odysseus and the Trojans.'

Alexander didn't reply, he sat up, got out of bed naked and went out for a moment.

'Do you miss not having children?' he said when he reappeared in the doorway.

Words can be like small doses of poison. The dose slips from the tongue down the pharynx and throat, almost unnoticed. Apparently without effect, but after a while the stuff spreads. A little at first, and then a little more, until it paralyses the legs, the arms and the rest of the body and finally the head.

'It's what I wanted most of all,' I said. 'Leandros thought that the money he earned as an officer would enable us to buy a house and start a family in Pella. Neither of us could have known that your campaign would last forever. But you're getting away from what Priamos said.'

Alexander shrugged his shoulders.

'No one can deny your great talents on the battlefield,' I went on, 'but you know nothing about the wars and the armies here within the palace. You're putting us both in danger by not knowing where the battle lines are drawn.'

It's just as if Alexander hasn't left home yet. He hasn't been back to Pella for almost ten years, but he nearly always rambles about Olympias and Philip in his sleep. On numerous occasions I've been roused by shouts for his mother and father. It was like that last night, too. He awoke, emptied the wine jar and fell asleep again.

'Lanike!'

I shook him. I knew that was the name of his wet nurse, he'd told me about her several times. After a while I heard him again:

'Don't let me go, Father, don't!' he shouted. 'I'm drowning.'

'What is it?' I asked.

'I'm learning to swim.'

Alexander is said to have inherited Philip's sense of justice, his clear head and loyalty to ideas. In addition, he's a systematic and practical man. He's supposed to have got his passion and impetuosity from Olympias. That's what they say in the kitchens. If that's the case, it could only have been true before we settled in Babylon. All I know is that he still can't swim.

I lay gazing over at Alexander and tried to imagine what he'd looked like when he was twenty and had initiated his campaign against the Persians: his hair must have been thicker, his skin browner, his smile more frequent, his movements faster, his orders unhesitating. What a futile thought. The man by my side, who closes his eyelids and tilts his head a little more to the side, closer to me, is mine. I shall watch over and protect him, I thought. His father made him a soldier, a general and a king, but it's his mother who is his confidante, and I am too.

I awoke to Alexander shouting to the two guards outside for more wine.

'Alexander, is it true that your father believed he was a direct descendant of the son of Zeus, and that your mother still thinks she's related to Achilles?' I asked.

He looked at me in astonishment.

'Thinks?' he repeated.

'I've heard that Aristotle finds it odd.'

'Wait a moment,' he said, and fetched the scroll that lay on the marble table in the corner of the room.

He placed himself before me.

'Listen to what Mother writes about Aristotle, "He is so dry I can see the dust falling from him as he stands in the room."'

His face creased and he gave a long laugh.

He read and got a line by heart before looking over at me and reciting, 'My dear son, why can't the gods put all my wrinkles on the soles of my feet?'

'Not bad, eh?'

I nodded. He seated himself on the buffalo-skin divan, and drank from the flagon on the table.

'Or what about this, "In our family we don't divorce our spouses, we bury them."'

Alexander read a bit further down the scroll, 'I've bought a goodly quantity of strychnine.'

'What's that?' I asked as I wielded a palm fan to waft away the flies that buzzed around his body.

'It's a herb grown in the Indus valley, which can be useful for killing in an unobtrusive way.'

'An unobtrusive way?'

'Aristotle has named the herb *Strychos nuxvomica*. Talk about something else, Phyllis. Forget what I said.'

'At home, my father said that Philip united the Greek city states?'

'You should have seen just how much my father feared me. Once he realized that I was capable of excelling him both as a king and a military leader, he attempted to elevate my brother Arrhidaeus to outrank me. Arrhidaeus who couldn't even speak, and who dribbled the whole time.'

'He's like my sister Agrippa. She's sweet in her way, but not suited to doing . . .'

I thought better of it. '—food.'

'Precisely, he doesn't know left from right, fish from fowl, mountains from sea. Father wanted him to marry the King of

Caria's daughter, just to humiliate me. I would have run my sword through Father, not once, but a hundred times.'

His eyes were glistening.

'Your father should have noted your strength and willpower when you tamed Bucephalus.'

Alexander nodded.

'He should have realized you'd become a seasoned warrior, and not just some boy who was content to take a bow and go sparrow-hunting. Every Macedonian knows that you crushed the Thebans' flank, and that it was decisive in our conquest of the city states.'

'So it was,' he shouted, got up, went to the door and ordered more to drink.

He sat down again. He began to cry and shake his head.

'Why couldn't Father be content, be happy, enjoy the acclaim, instead of allowing himself to be brought down by that eighteen-year-old Eurydice and to father a daughter, Europa, by her?'

'Did Philip go to your sister's wedding without his bodyguards?'

He raised his eyes.

'What are you saying?'

'You and Olympias might have thought that Philip felt himself unassailable in every way. Is it true that the assassin, Pausanias, had formerly been your father's lover? I've heard that three soldiers whisked the murderer off. Pausanias could hardly have foreseen that the three he thought were his allies, killed him a short distance from the celebrations. Isn't that right?'

'There you are,' Alexander exclaimed. 'Phyllis, you're clairvoyant! You can see into the future and the past. What else do you know?'

His face was smudged with tears. I got out of bed, picked up my turquoise tunic. He bowed his head. I began to talk:

'Washed in wine, your father's bones were consumed by the flames. Everything was burnt: his armour, his favourite weapons, Pausanias' dagger, the four slaughtered horses, and once they had turned to ash they were thrown on the burial mound.'

I could hear how eager I sounded, but I went on regardless:

'The following day, Eurydice, her newborn son, her uncle General Attalus, Pausanias' three sons and most of the people who hadn't voted for you in the royal election were executed.'

Alexander leapt to his feet, stood in front of me and shouted:

'You've been in my library, Phyllis!'

Alexander hit me, hard, with the flat of his hand. 'If you never mention the library to a living soul, I may, just possibly, refrain from killing you.'

'Lysimachus has to sleep sometimes. I just happened to tread on the third flagstone from the wall right behind your big bed, behind the crimson curtain, and a section of wall opened.'

He struck me another blow, to my head, I fell and shielded myself with my hands. I wasn't bleeding, my neck was sore.

'I found the speech you made at your father's funeral. The speech was brief and moving and was about how much the king had meant to you as a soldier, an officer and now as a king. "I shall pay homage to my beloved father by building a monument that will dwarf the Pyramid of Cheops."'

I lay on my side, raised my knees. My fingers, hands and arms protected most of my head in anticipation of further blows.

He made no reply. He lowered his arm.

'Antipater's career was dependent on my becoming king. I wanted to make him head of the army and ultimately, regent. My mother's life could have been at stake if I hadn't become king. There were plenty of heirs apparent. Lysimachus has his good points, he's certainly a good archivist, but he's no soldier. For some years he's been a conscientious librarian and looked after all the scrolls and copies of the things I sent to Aristotle. Say how you managed to get in.'

'The last time you and Roxane journeyed to Mesopotamia, I couldn't help myself. As soon as I'd finished my work, I knocked on the door of your room. Lysimachus answered. Most men become responsive after a few compliments, no matter how untrue they are. It's often more effective than a smile. I almost felt sorry for him when I praised his hair.'

'That's quite enough,' Alexander interjected.

Not only was Lysimachus the king's scribe but he also looked after the library in every city Alexander occupied during the campaign. And as Alexander moved further eastward across the world, at all times of year, in every kind of weather and terrain, Lysimachus guarded the three great wagons of scrolls and artefacts. Lysimachus is a thin, elderly man, bony, as if desiccated by too much walking by the wagons through innumerable deserts. Without a doubt, many people would have thought his work meaningless and incomprehensible, but I envied him. Not merely for the reading material he had access to but what of all the opportunities he had for discovering things about his king? I had to get Lysimachus out of the way quickly. 'Two new kinds of mushroom have arrived in the kitchens which no one's seen before. The king has asked you to take a look at them. You don't need to lock up. I'll stand guard!' I told him.

He hesitated momentarily before nodding and setting off. As he didn't know the shortcut from the king's apartments to the kitchens, I was confident I had a little time. I walked quickly through the library. The walls were the colour of ochre. The doors were white and had a square picked out in gold leaf in the middle. Duplicates of objects sent to Aristotle lay everywhere on tables and shelves: beetles, dried plants, as well as fish and animals in a liquid I didn't recognize, which prevented them from stinking. The smell in this library was odd to say the least. I couldn't help myself, and took a quick look at some scrolls about campaigns, defensive and aggressive, speeches and letters 'from Olympias', obviously the ones for public consumption, at least for the eyes of Lysimachus.

These weren't what I was looking for, but a little time remained before Lysimachus was due back. I pulled the curtain aside and trod on the tile which made the door open. This room had two openings in the wall. They allowed me to see reasonably well. Inside it was bereft of exhibits and the air was much purer. The titles I managed to glimpse on scrolls were: 'Useful Tortures for Finding the Way to the Next Village'; 'The Plans the Gods Have for Me'; 'Dreams I've Never Shared with Anyone'; 'Fantasies, Hephaestion' (I managed to unroll this and ascertain that the fantasies were very explicit); 'The Weather and Other Things Forecast by Birds in the Morning'; 'The Truth About Father's Death'; 'Why Looking at Constellations Makes Me Feel the Loss of Animals and People I Have Known'; 'The Effects of a Vessel's Wake on the Mood of Dolphins'; 'Languages I Have Helped to Eradicate, Either by Killing the Last Native Speaker, Or by Prohibition'; 'On the Correlation Between Echoes and the Moon'; 'Aristotle's Lack of Practical Skill with Horses', to which he'd added the subtitle, 'He's Never Ridden One At All'; 'A Horse's Thoughts About Winds of All Strengths and from All Directions; Grass: Thin, Thick, Tall, Short; Grass Facing North, West, South, East, Scorched, Fresh, etc.' was the longest title I saw.

I found a scroll with my own name on it, together with those of Roxane and Barsine, grabbed it and read 'Phyllis' right foot and toes are an imitation of a hand from another world and possess a peculiar beauty'.

I tore out the part that referred to me and tried to rip it to shreds. It was more difficult than I'd imagined. The papyrus was strong and resilient. I threw the scroll behind a stack of firewood.

I became apprehensive and hurried to the door leading to the passage. Lysimachus was making his way up the last, long flight of stairs. I was just about to make a run for it when I realized he'd met someone he obviously knew, and they were conversing cordially.

My eye fell on a scroll of odd sketches. It was called 'Morning sketches'. Another was called, 'Drawings of animals I haven't sent to Aristotle', with detailed captions detailing anatomy, mating, behaviour, size and weight. A scroll entitled 'A Study of Colours' was an orderly review of the effect colours have on each other as follows: black–gold–black, gold–white– silver, and green–orange–violet, but I wasn't able to work out its significance.

No, I'm not clairvoyant, not even when I warned Alexander against you, Antipater. The fact that Alexander's parents made him believe in his own divinity, reduced his ability to spot dangers we others have to be wary of to survive. Just as I was about to close the door to the library, I saw the Antipater scroll. I hope you realize that it's one of the largest scrolls. I satisfied myself that Lysimachus was still talking at the bottom of the stairs, unrolled it and began reading. I discovered nothing I hadn't heard before, apart from his name for you, 'the old goat'. It's scarcely a telling vilification as you're an elderly gentleman with a characteristic beard. The tone is generally anxious and respectful. Alexander is literally scared of you. You know too much about one another. You've been his most loyal supporter. Until now. Everything written about you is suffused with admiration and tinged with gratitude. In describing you, words like 'courage' and 'loyalty' constantly crop up. Just think how close you both were twelve years ago, when Alexander began his conquests. According to my calculations you are the same age as Philip would have been. No one taught Alexander more about the arts of war and strategy than you did. Alexander and his father must have underestimated your ambition. You'll survive them both. You were justifiably incensed when Philip forbade you to take part in putting down the Greek city states. Instead, you were ordered to stay at home with Prince Alexander.

I just managed to get out as Lysimachus was coming in. Clearly irritated, he announced that the mushroom in the kitchen was well known and perfectly common.

Leandros was what most women would call 'a good husband', thoughtful, kind and loving, in the sense that he was generous with tender words. It's said that women should be thankful when their husbands don't beat them. The same applies to donkeys, who ought to be docile and obedient when their owners don't use the whip. Like Plato, I believe that women ought to expect more than donkeys. As soon as the king landed in Asia, after crossing the Dardanelles, he hurled a spear into the dry ground.

'This is Troy!' Alexander roared.

'How do you know it's here?' Hephaestion enquired.

'Well, call it *Alexander's* Troy then,' the king commanded.

Alexander gave instructions for the erection of altars to Zeus, Athene and Heracles.

'Why isn't Antipater here?' one of the generals asked.

'Don't concern yourself about that,' said Alexander.

I know all this because Leandros was standing close by when the orders were given.

Another ten years were to pass before Alexander and I met.

We were barely twenty years old when we stood on Asian soil for the first time. The army totalled 48,100 men, according to Leandros. In addition, Alexander had 160 warships under his command and about one hundred transport vessels. The crews amounted to almost 38,000 men. Then there were all of us army followers: scholars, historians, artisans, cooks, weapon makers, tailors, hunters to procure food, smiths, a few officers' wives, cup-bearers, victory-feast organizers, engineers, architects, more than 100,000 in all.

There weren't many of us women when we went ashore in Asia, maybe a hundred all told. Alexander and his generals had the idea that the women would run Macedonia and the Greek states while they were away. But who was going to empty the latrines, wash the floors and clothes, play lyres and flutes, go to bed with the soldiers and look after them when both legs had been amputated or their eyes had been gouged out? The need for the women in the rearguard became apparent only a few days after landing. I saw it at close quarters. We Macedonian and Greek women were soon in the minority compared to the thousands of Persian women who'd been taken prisoner. They remained with the expedition. This meant children. It is unbelievable that Alexander and the military command hadn't foreseen this.

Everyone was surprised that the Persian king, Darius, and the Persian army, even larger than our own, weren't waiting for us when we landed. After three days, some scouts discovered that Darius had left Babylon with his entire treasury, his family, his concubines and all their baggage as soon as we'd set foot on Anatolian soil.

We marched south. We took Lydia without a fight. Everywhere the natives fled and let us conquer one city after the other. At the mere mention of Alexander's name, they ran. Every one of us assumed a power we'd never had before. I felt strong and invincible. We were the master race, and those we came up against knew they'd be beaten whether they fought us or not. Weeks later, at Myriandrus, we made camp. The Persians waited a day's march away. One day, two days, then on the fourteenth day, during a tremendous rainstorm, the Persian army of 75,000 men marched towards us. We were 30,000 all told. Darius sent word that he would meet our army on the great, open plain near Sokhoi. Alexander urged patience on Leandros and all his brother officers. He knew that we had to stay as close to the coast as possible in order to get supplies by sea from the north. But Darius' army made a detour and attacked the town of Issus, where Alexander had left his sick and wounded to recuperate. The city fell, almost without resistance. Darius gave orders that the prisoners' hands were to be cut off before they were sent back to us. The sight of our mutilated soldiers enraged us. General Kharios made a speech to us followers, and the amputees. He called Darius 'pathetic, cowardly, overblown scum'. Some died of loss of blood but many were saved, thanks to a surviving field hospital and the efforts of countless women. Many of the maimed were sent home, in despair at being unable to avenge themselves.

The battle was fought on the narrow coastal strip. The evening before the attack Alexander said we were going to meet one of Asia's weakest tribes, 'In addition, you'll have me as leader in the fight against Darius.' During the battle he shouted orders to his men by name, not only the generals but also the squadron commanders and even the captains. My husband never forgot the way he roared, 'Leandros, I know that you're a model to your men. Forward now, don't hang back, you are unconquerable.' They crushed the Persian army and captured the queen and the queen mother as Darius fled like a frightened rat. Alexander commandeered Darius' carriage which housed his treasury containing countless gold coins; not content with that he confiscated Darius' gilded bath and carried it with him wherever he went.

Antipater, there are many people who'd like to see Alexander dead. You, Roxane, Aristotle and several of the Greco-Macedonian military, to name but a few.

Roxane has every reason to hate her husband. Aristotle perceives that his pupil is in the process of creating a kingdom in which Greek hegemony is under threat. Alexander's old friends among the generals are war-weary and believe their prestige is being lost to Persian and Indian soldiers.

Perhaps Admiral Nearchus is the only one without a motive. He needs Alexander. He knows that the other military leaders are either sceptical about, or in deep disagreement with the plans for conquering Arabia. Nearchus knows that should Alexander die, his ambition and his opportunity to court public opinion would be in tatters. 'Wherever there's the stink of blood, Nearchus wants to be there,' Alexander said of his admiral. 'He's like some wild dog.'

I picture the river in the Pella of my childhood. A wild boar cavorts on its oddly stiff legs, high-backed and black against the white sand of the riverbank. The boar tries to avoid the water and runs away from it, but is surrounded by dogs. Droplets fly from its thin coat. The dogs bark frantically, steam rises from them. The boar turns as the first dog comes up. It twists and thrusts. The dogs throw themselves on its hind-quarters, the animal circles and attacks them with its tusks. It must retreat, but stops when it sees the river behind it and kicks its back legs in the air. Finally, it manages to drive a tusk into the belly of one dog, tears it open and the intestines well out. This doesn't deter its other attackers. Two of them get hold of one of its back legs, another clamps its jaws around the boar's throat. Whitish-grey mud and sand swirl. Gushing blood makes lines and arcs like black writing in the sand. One dog gets hold of its ear. Two others are down, one crawls away whining, but the three remaining dogs force the boar down and kill it.

A voice I recognized only too easily could be heard outside the room. A voice that rose above all the others. Roxane assuring herself that the soldiers were watching that I didn't escape. Patiently, they told her that I'd shown no desire even to try. How could Alexander bear to kiss that mouth?

I screamed. I shouted her name. Two soldiers came running in and threw me on the floor. Roxane was behind them.

'Feel your belly, you're carrying a serpent beneath your breast, you couldn't give birth to anything else.'

'Kill her, don't you hear what she's saying?' Roxane yelled.

She tried to grab hold of my hair. The guards hustled her out. I shouted. The men stopped my mouth until everything went black.

I awoke on the floor, alone.

The door opened slowly. I was frightened that Roxane was returning. It was a relief to see Zara, my half Persian, half Greek assistant from the kitchens. She came with food, and looked behind her quickly to make sure the guards couldn't hear. Cabbage soup was placed on the table.

'Even I can see that the king hasn't got more than a couple of days left,' she whispered. 'He's foaming at the mouth. I see it when I bring food to those who watch over him.'

The guards shouted for her, she stroked my hair quickly, before leaving with my slops bucket. Perhaps that would be the last time I'd receive anything like a caress, I thought as the door shut behind her.

Soon there'll be a thousand people clustering around the main entrance to the palace. It's certainly no parade. Private soldiers are in evidence, too, and people who aren't normally allowed there. Our new rulers have no control. There is shouting. Horns are being blown. What an uproar. Now they're chanting, 'Alexander!' The people outside haven't forgotten that Alexander has risen from the dead before. Three years ago when the Mallians were defending their city walls, he ordered his men to set up ladders and climb over. They refused. So he stormed up the rungs himself, with only three companions. It was lethal and pointless. Alexander leapt down the other side and was met by a hail of arrows. A shaft penetrated his chest. He collapsed. Peucestas, Alexander's personal bodyguard, laid his shield over his body and continued fighting. At the last moment the Macedonians managed to force the city gate. The king's lifeless body was carried out to safety. The barbs of the long arrow had penetrated his breastbone. That's what I've heard, but I've never been given any plausible explanation about how he survived.

Here the text contains several illegible words and a long crossing out. With hindsight, and using sources such as Diodorus and Plutarch—who are almost identical—I can provide the following sequence of events:

An army surgeon managed to extract the arrow but the loss of blood had been considerable. One of the lungs had been punctured. A froth of blood and air bubbled out of the wound in the chest at each breath. The soldiers, who such a short time before had been incensed at the king's foolhardiness, were now beside themselves with agitation that Alexander might die of his injuries. A rumour started that without the king's help, they would never get home. When Alexander regained consciousness, he dictated a letter that was meant to set his soldiers' minds at rest. It had the opposite effect. They were convinced that the king was dead and that the letter was an attempt to deceive them. The king was placed in the prow of a boat which sailed past them. The men

*wept, certain that a corpse was floating by on the mirror-calm
water. Alexander gave his attendants orders to procure a horse.
The boat was moored. With great effort, Alexander succeeded in
walking ashore. He managed to mount the horse by sheer willpower and to ride through the camp, through a rain of flowers and
wild cheering.*

*When Alexander returned to his bodyguards he was exhausted,
and two of the strongest men lifted the king off his horse and carried him into his tent.*

*This is how the tale is told by historians today, and by those
of the medieval and ancient world. They all draw on the descriptions of Callisthenes. None of them has posed any questions or
challenged this narrative, no matter how implausible it seems. I
haven't either.*

*They say that cats have nine lives. Alexander had nine hun-
dred. He managed to cheat death every time, according to his
chroniclers. But not in Babylon.*

❧

The shouts from outside are increasing in volume. The soldiers and the crowd here in Babylon have pushed past the bar-
rier and its guards. Again and again they demand assurances
that Alexander is still alive.

The vast majority of people I've observed alter when they
see the king in his audience chamber. They tense, they stammer; their words, if they come at all, pour out helter-skelter.

Some are disappointed that he isn't taller. When they see how many servants and soldiers obey him, and the authority with which he gives his orders, their expectations are largely fulfilled. Sometimes Alexander gets tired of being stared at. The embarrassing thing about these gawpers is that they don't realize that they're the ones being looked at. In Alexander's present condition he has ample opportunity of enjoying the sport. Their looks are sharp enough to whittle flesh away from the tiniest facial bone. Many of them say that meeting the king will give them extra strength; they have met the most important man in the world, a man who's been turned into a god.

Some out there are weeping, soldiers, officers, market crones, bakers, even peasants have come to stand in front of the entrance. I can't tell if they seem expectant, but they're silent, perhaps dubious is nearer the mark. Now a few of them have begun to call the queen's name. Those who shout are pushed away.

'Send the Persian whore home,' they yell. 'Kill her,' others shout. They're unconcerned that Roxane may be standing at her husband's side and might be able to hear them. The guards and sentries are more cautious than Alexander would have been. He would have ordered the Royal Squadron to clear the agitators. A shouted order tells the people they must move back. They obey.

Last night I heard a voice in the darkness. It troubles me that even now I don't understand who was talking to me. Even though I don't believe in gods, I do take dreams seriously. The voice said:

'The gods have shaped the human body. It slowly dies and turns to dust. Dreams don't decompose. When human beings worship gods, they worship them as miracles. I do not wish to be worshipped. You fear doubt and fantasy. If you want to give me a name, call me Sister of the Sun and Moon, the ruler of dreams. I don't insist on existing, as the other gods of the world do, but I'm always close by when imagination burgeons, when doubt arises and invisible libraries are under construction. When one hand doesn't know what the other is doing, I am there.'

It has been four days since I was brought here. If I'd been an ordinary prisoner, I'd be rotting in one of the dungeons. The knowledge that what I am writing is the last thing I'll ever do, gives me extra strength. The sound of angry voices woke me just now. Crowds of people are continually arriving on the parade ground outside. Delegations of every colour are constantly emerging. Those waiting run towards them. The people shout impatiently at one another. An officer places himself before them.

'Alexander lives!' he cries.

Several of those waiting to be let in, shake their heads, some demand shrilly how he knows that. Even this far away I can hear someone say that he thought the king whispered something to him.

Zara from the kitchen has just been in with more soup and the empty bucket.

'They say the king is ill because he spent so much time in the swamps of the Euphrates valley recently. Some think the insects have made him ill,' she said.

'So it's not fatal?'

She shook her head energetically.

'The king has smiled and blinked his eyes.'

Zara didn't hear my sigh.

Alexander can't make offerings to the gods any more. No matter how drunk, sick or exhausted he was, he offered food to Zeus and Apollo. I've often wondered how he knew what the gods liked. I can't fathom, for example, how he could be so sure that Apollo liked oily fish and wine. Even though the servants who tend the palace hearths volunteered to make the morning offerings, he insisted on doing it himself because he wanted to speak directly to the gods.

He gets no help from Roxane at all. She does nothing to please our gods. Despite Alexander's respect for her gods, customs and festivals, she does nothing in return.

Alexander and I appreciated the beauty of our childhoods' Pella keenly, but Babylon became our favourite city of all. It wasn't just its size but as Alexander said so often during our first evening walking about, 'It's as if Babylon was built block by block, square by square, palace by palace, house by house, street by street, pillar by pillar, garden by garden, flower by flower, to a carefully preconceived plan, a homage to beauty.'

When we left Ecbatana, after the bonfire of Hephaestion's remains had burnt out, Alexander hadn't much faith in the welcome the population of Babylon would give him. On the previous occasion, eight years earlier, he'd been a hero in Babylonian eyes because he'd beaten the Persians at the battle of Gaugamela. Alexander had been a liberator, he'd given them the belief and the expectation of greater self-determination. Now, he was unprepared for their anger. It seemed that their treasurer, Harpalos, his own appointee, was corrupt.

He's simply lost command and control. Priamos told me that Alexander had consulted nine astrologers about which direction he ought to enter Babylon so as not to arouse the gods' displeasure. I refused to believe my boss. The last time Alexander and I went out after dark, I asked if the story were true.

'They said that if I rode into the city from the east, things might be all right,' he replied.

'So the army had to make a huge detour to the north until they got to the road the Babylonian astrologers thought was right?'

'Speak more softly, Phyllis.'

'To think, you, the conqueror of the world, being shown where to enter your own capital. The son of Zeus has fallen far.'

'I listened to them so as not to make more enemies in the city here. I've got enough problems with the treasurer.'

Alexander and I thought we'd left the palace unnoticed. Darkness had just fallen. Roxane had been in bed for more than a week, fearful she might lose her baby. He suggested we look around the city. I thought it would be safer to use the little temple for our assignations. I was worried we'd be found out.

'Roxane's got other things on her mind,' he said.

He was patting and stroking me as if I'd had a fleece and wings, as if he'd discovered some exotic animal.

The last time the army had been in Babylon, Alexander occupied the palace. I lived outside the walls of the city with Leandros, in the camp built by the Macedonian army beyond the city gate. I would never have seen Babylon if it hadn't been for Alexander.

He was dressed in a tunic without too many ornaments and marks of rank. I'd finished work for the day.

Alexander and I never tired of admiring the splendour before our eyes as we wandered up and down the great thoroughfares of Babylon, as lovers had done for a thousand years before us. We strolled among the stalls in the market where they sold flowers, fish of every colour and size, mackerel, tuna and red mullet, there were even eels, scallops and mussels from the Mediterranean, prawns, crabs, lobsters and oysters, I raised an open oyster to my lips and swallowed the contents. Such a light, metallic taste with a tang of the sea. Alexander showed me the hard shell that encloses the soft body within. I saw elephant tusks and rhinoceros horns, live animals and dead animals, gold, diamonds, cloth from every corner of the world, fruits: grapes, apples, figs, prunes and vegetables I'd never seen before, spices and rare herbs. At one stall Alexander tried out a lyre, his favourite instrument, before inspecting the quality of some linen shirts hanging next to beautiful abacuses and wax-covered tablets. He was unstoppable: hip-baths of terracotta, cypress and olive-wood furniture, and papyrus rolls were all carefully scrutinized before he hastened off to another stall. He was like a child with the new toy he'd thought he'd never get.

Like most other people, we processed through the Ishtar Gate, that magnificent door in the city wall made of glazed bricks of every conceivable colour. In the evening light it was as if the scents from the Hanging Gardens inside the gate smelt extra heady. The gardens towered eighty feet into the air. Which other city greets you in this way, with all the flowers of the world? Alexander said that the flowering trees had been planted by the royal gardener on Nebuchadnezzar's orders. They came from Queen Semiramis' native land. On both sides of the main street, 'Let not the enemy prevail', are raised terraces planted with trees and climbers kept green and colourful with water pumped up from wells and invisible springs beneath the street and the beds. The watering system sends jets in all directions and sprays droplets that satiate the petals and yellow styles of white, pink, red and ruby flowers, before they run down leaves and stems and reach the rich, dark earth the plants are grown in. As we smelt the scents and heard the water spraying and the buzz of voices approaching and receding on both sides of the street, we were still within sight of the Ishtar Gate, named after the Babylonian goddess of love. The towers on either side were almost twice as high as the gate. It's strange to think that this is the same street I can see from here, and that lovers are strolling up and down this evening, as if nothing has happened.

We could see the great temple of Esagila, shaped like a pyramid and dedicated to the people's tutelary deity.

'It was here that Marduk, the god of the Persians, came down from the sky to meet his people,' Alexander said. 'This building is the biggest and tallest in the world. I'm not sure just how many storeys it has.'

It terrified me because I couldn't comprehend how human hands had built this thing towering into the sky. Had it been built by unknown gods? Alexander pointed and said:

'I'm annoyed that some of our compatriots are patron-izing about the Babylonians' faith. They ought to show respect; they should at least realize, just looking at this edifice, how important religion is to the natives.'

We strolled past the temple, the houses stood packed together on both banks of the Euphrates. Palaces and lesser temples had been built among them. Alexander said that more than a quarter of a million people lived behind these solid city walls.

Never again shall we see such beauty, or walk through the city imagining that life is there just for us.

On the main thoroughfare, after darkness had fallen, walked slaves with their owners, temple workers, apprentices, journeymen, foremen and masters of every conceivable trade. There were bakers, joiners, shipbuilders, coppersmiths, canal diggers, tailors, coopers, gravediggers and bird-catchers with their wives and sweethearts. Camels, donkeys and mules criss-crossed the street, carrying wares from the great market to one of the fine houses. 'It beats Pella', was a constant refrain between us, and then we'd giggle. Our native city was a village by comparison.

Alexander said that the streets weren't just thronged with Babylonians but also peoples I'd never heard of: Hittites, Kassites, Assyrians, Aramaeans, Chaldeans, Heratites and Elamites. A caravan from Baghdad with fifty-six camels and more than three times as many attendants in white tunics, passed down the middle of the road, as vendors and beggars stormed towards them. The majority of the houses were built around enclosed courtyards, with just one door on to the street. As the sun set, most of the inhabitants would climb to the roofs of the houses to pray to their god.

It would have been quite something to see all those flat roofs at once. Was it possible to walk from roof to roof in the quarter that lay nearest the Euphrates? Over at the great Bel temple, were a priest and an astronomer studying the moon to see what the following day would bring?

It was exciting to see the colours of the women's dresses and tunics. They wore thin leather sandals with gold or silver straps. The most popular colours were saffron-yellow, all shades of red, and violet. The girls had long hair, often in curls. The married women preferred their hair up. I had mine up too, so as not to stand out too much.

I wondered how I looked by Alexander's side, as we dallied in the most sublime of all cities.

'I've never been so happy,' I said.

It was very hot. The scent of the flowers hung heavy. Darkness had fallen. We were standing in front of a house where, in a parlour on the ground floor, women were made up and had their hair dressed. Alexander looked about to make sure no one was following. Not a single bodyguard or valet was with us or in the vicinity. Two aides, I shan't mention names, had shown us a secret tunnel leading out of the palace. Alexander was wearing a turquoise tunic, and I had an ankle-length, saffron-yellow dress. We thought we were beautiful. We told each other so. I was wearing earrings and bracelets of gold and silver. An elderly woman asked if I wanted my hair done. I said yes. Alexander introduced us as a married couple who made clothes for the Macedonian army.

Two women washed my hair, dried it with towels and curled it with tongs. Then my face was treated with oils and creams before they started putting make-up around my eyes and mouth. It's the custom to paint the top and sides of the eyes like the Egyptian women.

Alexander waited for me in the street. He inspected me thoroughly, then he kissed me.

'Give up the kitchens, and be my wife.'

'Is that an order? You've got a wife and soon you'll have a child.'

'My father had seven. Mother and Roxane will have to accept it.'

'But will Aristotle accept it?'

'I am king. Be with me, every day.'

I ran my fingers over his hairy arm.

'Athens' greatest man, Pericles, had a consummate love, originally a whore . . .'

He paused momentarily.

' . . . who became his speechwriter and his wife.'

'Are you talking to me or to a whore?' I said, and felt the tears welling.

He looked around. I noticed that I couldn't see out of one eye. My fingers were black with make-up. I glanced up at his face again. He didn't move. He stood there.

We should have vanished into the crowd, for the kingdom's sake and our own. Alexander was separated from the blind loyalty of his guards, who were trained to shield him with their own bodies against attacks from axes, swords, knives or deadly arrows. The crush in Babylon's main thoroughfare is the ideal spot for assassination, using a knife for example. An unknown passer-by can easily stab low down, and pull the blade upward. There are knives so sharp that you can walk several yards before you realize what's happened. They say that the initial sensation is of a sudden burning. Soon after, the stinging develops into pain between the lower ribs, and then the eyes take in the black patch on the clothing which spreads rapidly downward from the stomach. By the time the smell of blood reaches the nostrils, life is ebbing away.

Alexander stood there with me. He held out his arms. He clasped me. One of the women who'd attended to me, came running out. She took me by the arm and began mopping me with a perfumed flannel, cleaned away the make-up and deftly reapplied the ruined lines above my eyes.

Alexander took me by the arm and led me along the great canal. We strolled across the bridge, below which sailing barges moved through the darkness, the voices on board floating up to us. We reached an eating house where the ingredients were hanging up outside the door. One of the dishes was called 'well-hung fillet of King Darius'. A man outside chased inquisitive dogs away and tried to entice hungry patrons in. We looked at each other, nodded. There was a vacant table at the back of the large premises. It smelt good, and it looked clean. We sat down and ordered quails as an appetizer. Alexander asked if they had wild boar. The waiter shook his head. We had to make do with hare. For pudding we had grapes and pears with honey.

'D'you often think of the son you had with Barsine?' I asked.

It came out sounding rather abrupt.

'How often have you seen him?'

He emptied his cup.

He ordered more to drink.

'What do you think about the child in Roxane's womb?'

He reacted with a grimace.

'It must end well and it must be a boy, or else it'll be like some great, lost battle,' he actually used that word, 'for Macedonia and the world.'

I waited to see if he was going to say any more.

He inhaled:

'The child in Roxane's belly isn't mine, but Macedonia's.'

As he said it, it was as if he'd laid bare a small unknown part of himself which was normally concealed in that powerful, scarred man's body. He shut his eyes.

'But,' I said out loud, 'I've always wanted to have a child with you.'

'Don't you realize what would happen? Roxane would have you killed before a day had passed.'

A waiter came up behind me and cleared the table. Alexander opened his eyes, looked at me kindly and took my hand:

'Let's go and see an entertainment that's showing at the end of Paradise Street.'

He paid, took me gently by the arm and led me out.

A woman and a man, and a large bull with terrifying horns, were performing in a big tent. The woman, clad in red trousers and top, was barefoot. She placed herself directly in front of the enraged bull which pawed the sand and snorted before charging her. The man, who was dressed in black, ran following its tail. Just as the animal lowered its head to skewer her, she leapt straight up, grabbed hold of its horns, swung herself over the beast's back and was caught by the man running behind. The bull raged on tossing its horns in thin air several times, much to the public's amusement. I was sitting so close I could see the beads of sweat on the young woman's brow.

'It usually ends well,' Alexander said.

The blonde woman didn't smile as the applause broke out, and the bull, which still must have been wondering what had become of her, was guided out by ten men armed with long, iron-spiked poles.

Just as the clapping died down, Alexander turned quickly. A short woman stood behind us. I'd never seen her before. Alexander said that she was Roxane's lady-in-waiting. When the woman realized she'd been discovered, she rose, pushed past the nearest people in the crowd and began to run. I wasn't scared about her reporting to Roxane that we were lovers. She'd heard such things before. More serious was the fact that she'd seen Alexander's confidence in me, that we'd been talking and laughing together as friends. She could claim that we'd been talking about anything—about politics, about military matters, that I'd been exploiting his weaknesses, and that I was in the process of destroying the realm from within. I begged Alexander to run after her, I implored him to kill her.

'Don't you understand?' I asked anxiously.

'Well, what if she does tell Roxane and really lays it on thick, who can the queen go to?'

We got home unobserved and went to our own separate wings. I locked the door of my room and placed a bench in front of it, so that I'd wake up if anyone came and be able to defend myself with the knife under my pillow. My disquiet wasn't lessened when Alexander wouldn't share his bed with me that night, because he wanted to talk to Roxane.

Large, dark swarms of people move back and forth on the main street beyond the parade ground. I stand in front of the opening in the wall and imagine I can hear that noisy multitude, borne on thousands of feet, moving through the city. I stand there thinking that the people constitute two torrents, each with its own direction, dark expressions, sly looks, broken conversations and a wave of gossip.

The night sky lies like a vault above the city. The air is easy to breathe. The light from the moon and stars casts a veil over the trees.

Only high fever or a serious illness can restore my ability to sleep soundly. It would be a release. As soon as I lie down on the bunk, my head fills with troubling thoughts, they multiply, they have thin skins that fill and swell, twining around, over and under each other, turning into snakes.

Zara enters with a bowl of something she says is fish soup.

I first heard Aristotle mentioned by Lysimachus' slave, the man who taught me to read at home in Pella. Once, after he'd finished reciting the final part of Sophocles' *Oedipus the King*, I asked him who he thought was the wisest person in Greece. He answered without hesitation: Aristotle.

I was happy in Pella and I could see the orchards and vineyards on the hillsides, and Mount Vermion in the distance. Unlike Aristotle, Lysimachus and his slave had nothing against teaching girls. They taught several other girls of my age. As far as I know, Aristotle has nothing against Sappho's poetry. But surely, even she had to learn to read and write? We heard about Homer, Achilles, Odysseus and the other heroes. Those were magical moments when he read from the *Iliad*, told us about Achilles and pointed on the map to where the most important events had taken place. Troy and the Peloponnese of the Achaeans were brought to life for us. What we were never taught was the history of Socrates' and Plato's philosophy. Leandros instructed me in that when we lived together. The boys were trained in the arts of war, and I envied them; but we girls learnt astronomy, rhetoric, medicine, geometry, zoology and botany, just as they did.

When Alexander spoke of Aristotle, it was as if he was transported. He believed everything Aristotle said. It was Aristotle who'd taught him that beyond the Hindu Kush lay the sea and the world's end. When the army marched into India and we advanced slowly towards the mountain chain in the distance, he repeated Aristotle's words as if they'd been spoken by a prophet—no, a god. When snowstorms and cold threatened to kill us, he shouted the words again. And when the starving and exhausted soldiers asked how he could be so sure, he replied that it was because Aristotle had taught him it was true. Leandros shouted out that Aristotle had never been here. At first Alexander made no reply, but when others joined in, and even began screaming at him, he answered that Aristotle had calculated that they'd see the ocean on the other side of the mountains.

Yet again Alexander managed to persuade his men to march on. The rest of us followed because we had no choice. Alexander and his soldiers negotiated the Hindu Kush through a pass where a thousand died of cold and hunger. We others went along the valley, but after seventy days of rain and snow we finally reached the River Hyphasis. There, Alexander and his army were in for another shock. The king had told us that we should behold a tranquil sea, pleasantly warm, its waters every shade of blue and green. From there we'd be able to sail home, for the sage had taught Alexander that too. Then the task would be over. We'd have conquered the world.

What had once been the Macedonian army was now a force comprising a myriad of peoples: Greeks, Egyptians, Persians, Indians and races whose names I can't even pronounce any more. We had defeated the Persians and Indians, the ones who'd ruled this part of the world. There were no woods or trees on the banks of the Hyphasis to obscure the view. East of the river lay an endless stretch of plain, on the further side of which rose the vast Himalaya, as if poured down from the sky.

There was no sea. There was no Oceanos, as Aristotle had predicted. Alexander thought that mist was to blame, and that next morning it would lift. Next morning arrived, and there was no change. The Himalayas had beaten Alexander. The king had lost to the mountains.

It snowed for sixteen days. The rations had been consumed. Around me I could see tracks in the snow. Aimless ciphers. The wind chiselled scars into the snowdrifts. I lay down. The crust prevented me from sinking into the snow. The cavalry was way ahead of us. The night, with golden nails hammered into its black sky, stretched above us. We were twelve who lay down on the snow to let death liberate us. We lay side by side. After a while the stars vanished. Suddenly the words of one of Sappho's poems came to me:

> The silver moon is set;
> The Pleiades are gone;
> Half the long night is spent, and yet
> I lie alone.

In vain, I repeated the words to myself to distract my mind from the pangs of hunger.

For seven days, we'd eaten nothing but plants and twigs we'd found under the snow and ice.

No enemy is stronger than cold, hunger and exhaustion. We hoped that sleep would carry us off. We held each other's hands. Two wounded soldiers who'd been given up by the medical corps were the only men among us. Four children of Greek fathers and Persian mothers already slept. In the moonlight, I caught sight of two soldiers I hadn't noticed before. Their hands and fingers resembled desiccated birds' claws. One was dead, the other moaned so loudly that I was again reminded of the hunger gnawing at my guts. The four mothers stroked their children's heads. I couldn't see if they were crying. An elderly woman, a latrine cleaner, was dead. She was the only one who had no hand to hold. Her arms were crossed over her chest.

I got on all fours and began to scratch through the snow crust in the hope of finding something I could eat. Beneath the crust the snow was powdery. My fingers bled. I don't know how long I kept it up. My hands touched something firm. It didn't feel like rock or earth. I dug around the hard thing. The ice and snow came away. The stars shone. A horse's head came into view. It was well preserved under the snow. The whites of its eyes, surrounded by the dark hide, made it look as if it were alive. I tried to chew it. My teeth couldn't penetrate the flesh. The next morning, we managed to thaw the head in the sun. Three of us were alive still. The two women and I ate frantically all afternoon. One of them had some asafoetida in her pouch, a plant that was new to me. Botanists who'd accompanied the army had taught her that eating some of this plant prevented stomach problems when digesting raw meat. When we'd eaten and were ready to go, we placed the corpses closer together in the sun, so that its rays could melt the dusting of new snow that covered them. Then we walked in the direction we thought the army lay.

I had finished my work by the middle of the day. I got ready quickly, with make-up and perfume Alexander had given me. We were to go out into the city together, in daylight for once. Roxane was on a visit to Opis. I was looking forward to it. The bodyguards outside the king's apartments had been told I was coming. I'd never been there during the day. I was shown into the hall where guests usually waited. No one else was there. After a short while he appeared, freshly bathed, but unshaven. That was unusual. He kissed me, he smelt nice, but his breath stank of wine.

'Have you been drinking?'

'No . . . yes, but that was last night.'

'When Nearchus was here?'

'Well, you know, we began talking about how we might attack Arabia.'

'Don't tell me you were discussing "military affairs". We kitchen staff call it "hitting the bottle". Perhaps you didn't notice that I was helping to serve you, just a couple of rooms away, while you were discussing Arabia. I've never seen two men drink more.'

'I didn't realize you were taking it all in.'

'It was a loud conversation. You couldn't agree about distances in Arabia, the type of terrain, where the population was situated or how you'd find your way.'

'You're bluffing, Phyllis.'

'Nearchus tried to excite you by describing the riches you'd miss if you didn't attack.'

'That's true.'

'Besides, the Arabians haven't shown you any respect or sent a single deputation to Babylon to sue for a peace and loyalty pact.'

'How do you know that?'

'You gave Nearchus the go-ahead to enlarge the fleet. You even gave in to the admiral's suggestion of dismantling our Phoenician vessels, so that they could be transported overland and reassembled on the Euphrates, close to the palace.'

'Did I really say yes to that?'

'Surely you realize that the admiral has no interest in the good of the realm, only his own private wealth and free wine. Are you aware that you gave orders for ships to be built from cypress wood, and that the harbour at Babylon was to be extended to berth a thousand vessels? Even I can see that such plans will lead to revolt. After all, it's the army that has to defend the huge land masses that have been conquered.'

'The army will be pleased when I give them orders to take the areas around the Caspian Sea, where the Scythians live, and then march westward towards Rome and Carthage.'

'Nearchus has pinpointed your weakness and he's exploiting it. Despite his red admiral's tunic, he is and will remain a drunkard. You're the only one who isn't troubled by his permanently purple face.'

'Come on,' Alexander said, laying a hand on my shoulder. 'Let's go down to the harbour and then walk into the city.'

In the furthest corner of the shipyard an enormous ship was being built. Tall scaffolding stood on either side of what was to be the navy's largest vessel.

'This,' he said pointing, 'will have room for four hundred oarsmen, five hundred soldiers and six sails. This ship will lead the fleet that will conquer Arabia.'

Alexander spoke loudly and eagerly, just as he had when he he'd been the greatest of all soldiers. I just felt uneasy. Nearchus, of all people, was to be Alexander's closest ally in the next campaign.

'Phyllis, have you forgotten that we're going into town afterwards? I must go home and change first. Come with me. I want you to meet a unique woman,' Alexander said.

I looked at him quizzically, he smiled and went off to change. When he returned he was dressed like an ordinary Babylonian, in a green tunic and scuffed sandals.

'Who is this woman?'

'So, your curiosity's been aroused?'

He took my hand. We walked through the corridors past my room, and out, behind the kitchens to the little-used lane leading down to the Euphrates. I stopped suddenly. I was frightened.

'Have you forgotten the last time we were out in the city?'

In a steady voice, he said:

'It's been some time since you last saw the lady-in-waiting who followed us and told Roxane, hasn't it?'

I nodded.

'No one's following us,' he whispered.

I squeezed his hand and smiled.

As soon as we reached the main thoroughfares in the heart of the city, we walked to edge of the town centre. He teased and laughed while I fretted about who this unique woman could be.

'I'm saying nothing. Haven't I always kept my word?'

'How old is she?'

'My lips are sealed, but I can divulge that she's Persian.'

Just then he halted in front of a large stable.

'This must be it,' he said.

A pale, slender-limbed woman with reddish hair emerged. He held out a generous handful of coins. Her face lit up and she took them. I judged her to be about fifty, but fit for her years.

Alexander explained why he was there in a hopelessly clumsy Persian. She listened, without interrupting or supplying the words he was leaving out, then smiled and disappeared into the stable. A moment later, she returned with a black stallion. She then climbed onto the horse's back, with arms held straight, pressed the palms of her hands on each side of its backbone, and ran them up towards its neck and head. Neither of us had seen anything like it before. There the lean woman sat, telling Alexander that the general belief that horses' ailments lie in their legs, was wrong.

'They emanate from the back,' she announced loudly, and began massaging.

According to Alexander, the woman had formerly been King Darius III's adviser on the army's horses, when the Persians had ruled Babylon. I can't remember her name. The stallion clearly respected her. The animal was obviously in pain, but allowed her to continue. Eventually, we heard two loud clicks. She looked over at my amazed expression and smiled, and explained that the sound was caused by air moving in the joints. The horse whinnied. She patted it, jumped down and ordered Alexander to mount and feel its vertebrae, the way she had shown us.

Alexander hooked his arm through mine and led me to an eating house where we were met by several of his bodyguards. He was merry and in high spirits. They took us to a room where we would be alone. The waiters arrived with live fish, shellfish and other creatures from the sea. Some of them were new to us. The containers were painted turquoise inside to make the water look appealing. We rejoiced at the sight of a huge lobster.

'We'll have that,' Alexander said.

Two waiters bore it out to the kitchen.

'Have you seen them in their true element?' I asked.

'No,' he said at length.

'It's strange that you and Nearchus can't swim. No one I know is more eager to fantasize about what lives in the sea than you two. I've heard that most of the men Nearchus has recruited into the Royal Macedonian Navy have never been to sea before.'

The lobster was placed in front of us, rosy and beautiful. It was as if he hadn't heard what I said. We ate slowly, attentively. It was a large lobster cut in two. There was enough for both of us.

'I've never managed to conquer an ocean,' he said, looking straight ahead. 'But there's something that's almost as good.'

'What?'

'Eating a large lobster—the larger the better—it's like consuming a king, a king of the sea; look at the well-developed shell, the powerful tail and the two large, mismatched claws with serrated edges. A warrior in black, who becomes a king in red once he's cooked. His flesh has the fresh taste of the ocean, it lies lightly on the stomach and doesn't make one feel overfull.'

When we left it was raining. We stood under a tall fig tree. The trunk was black. Dry leaves lay beneath its thick boughs. I caught the suffocating smell of putrefaction. Behind the tree a large group of men appeared. There must have been a hundred and fifty of them. A stout rope was tied around the group. A laden, swaying camel led by a soldier in ragged clothes passed by. The prisoners were silent.

'Who are they?' I asked.

'I've no idea.'

One of the prisoners, a man with a deformed face sporting a large lump for a nose and an eye that was completely closed, broke free and ran towards Alexander. The three soldiers guarding the men were busy with one who was trying to beat up a fellow prisoner. The stink manifested itself as soon as he came near.

'I've seen you before,' he said in Greek.

'You most certainly have not,' Alexander replied disconcerted.

The eye was squeezed shut by the cheek, nose and forehead, or so it seemed. It didn't appear to be an injury, more like a disease. I couldn't look away and ignore it.

'You couldn't give a poor devil a morsel of food, could you, noble lady?'

'Get away from her,' Alexander said roughly.

'Wouldn't the lady like a shag, eh?'

Alexander hit him full in the face with his fist. The man sprawled, the back of his head in the dust. His good eye stared wildly at Alexander, as if he were in the middle of a nightmare. Blood ran from his nose.

The man tried to change position, but there seemed to be no coordination between his body and his legs.

I glanced at Alexander. He was incensed.

The prisoner fumbled for something beneath his filthy, ragged tunic. It turned out to be a short knife. He thrust it into his own throat. Blood spurted and hit Alexander in the face.

'Well, there now, you do possess a kind of honour,' Alexander shouted, before the soldiers came storming up and kicked the dying man away. I calmed him down, relieved that nobody had recognized him, and steered him out of the growing crowd.

'D'you know what my father used to say to me?' I said.

Alexander made no reply.

'If you think you see a giant, check the height of the sun, make sure it's not the shadow of a dwarf.'

When Roxane returned from Opis, Alexander forbade me to enter the royal suite. Priamos could relate that the king had given him orders to stock the room and the temple with flagons of wine, leaving them in places Alexander thought only he and Priamos knew about.

One afternoon in the kitchens a Phoenician dishwasher told us a tale that made me feel sick and uneasy. He said that a Thracian friend of his, a seaman, had accompanied the king down the Euphrates as part of his retinue, some weeks previously.

Close by the swamps, a gust of wind had caught Alexander's wide-brimmed hat. The fact that the Phoenician mentioned this detail made me prick up my ears and take serious note, few people had seen Alexander with his straw hat. It landed in the turbid water. It was quickly retrieved, but the bluish-white royal diadem, which was attached to it, had been dislodged and was hanging from some reeds. The seaman dived in, swam over to the diadem, put it round his head so that it wouldn't get wet, and swam blithely back to the royal barge where the king sat. Alexander had applauded, thanked him, bidden his servants dry the seaman, and given him a talent. For the seaman this must have represented about ten years' wages.

As they went ashore, one of the soothsayers accompanying the party said that it didn't augur well that the diadem had been worn by someone not of royal blood. Alexander turned quickly to his four bodyguards.

'Best to be on the safe side,' he said.

Before the sun went down the seaman's head had been severed from his body by Alexander's burliest bodyguard.

Is that the thanks we get, those of us who perform services for Alexander? Does he hate us because we think he's in our debt? Or has he become so insecure that he's placed his life in the hands of a gaggle of seers and greedy counsellors who surround and humour him? These are questions I've asked myself more and more frequently here in Babylon.

Plutarch says little about Alexander's months in Babylon. According to this biographer he drank an unconscionable amount and lived 'a dissolute life', but he doesn't touch on the reasons.

As an adult I discovered a painting by Hans Holbein the Younger from 1522. It shows a woman by the name of Phyllis and Alexander's teacher, Aristotle. Phyllis sits astride the philosopher's back. The illustration is dark grey on a greyish-white background. Of all philosophers, Aristotle has meant the most to me, both in terms of ethics and the understanding of science, philosophy and poetics. I found several pictures of Phyllis and Aristotle painted in various countries down the ages. What is remarkable about them out is how little clothing they're both wearing.

I began to investigate the blanks in the story, for which there are no dependable sources. Finding out what lay hidden became an obsession. To make progress I had to get inside Phyllis' head. It wasn't merely a good idea. It was absolutely necessary in order to expose the things that had been concealed. My investigations took my mind off the physical pain I was in. It was like being able to run again, to sweat and let my lungs heave for more and more air.

Alexander doesn't get up. There, in his audience chamber he is gawped at, surrounded by stares he cannot protect himself from.

I'm on my way to the dentist, I'm pondering the mystery of Plutarch's silence about Alexander's final days. Plutarch was a Greek, as were Herodotus and Thucydides. They saw themselves as the historians of Western civilization and, in their own estimation, on a superior plane to other races. Had Plutarch written so little about Alexander's stay in Babylon because the king's lifestyle might have made readers doubt that the Greeks really were a chosen people? I fall, the asphalt receives me, I'm incapable of rising from the pavement in Karl Johansgate. I lie in a heap. People rush up. They look at me. They talk among themselves. Some stroll off, some shake their heads. Human beings are supposed to walk upright. It's been that way for a long time. I ask people not to pull my arms. I tell them they're joined to my shoulders. I ask them not to tug at my legs. At last I manage to get on all fours. I fall over on to my side. My arms are trapped beneath my torso. I can't get up. I stare at the asphalt.

A pigeon trips past right in front of me. A burger bap lies just to my right. I look at the faces above me. I can't whistle. The small muscles in my face have deserted me. It's gone crooked. A woman stoops over me. Her eyes appraise me from behind green glasses. She announces that I'm drunk. I tell her that isn't what's wrong. I manage to raise the upper part of my body. I shout at her, 'If I was certain that injury makes one wise, I'd have thrown myself out of the fifteenth floor of the SAS Hotel.' She removes her glasses. She says I can say what I want. I advise her to get home before it gets dark.

I collapse on my back, like a man overcome, a conquered man. Countless wrestling bouts were organized to please Alexander. Once the winner had got the loser down, the king ran forward to see the expression on the beaten man's face.

A royal servant came down to the kitchens one morning:

'Come with me, the king's waiting for you.'

I glanced over at Priamos. He nodded.

'Should I change?'

The servant shook his head. 'No, it's urgent.'

I wiped my hands on my apron and left it on the work surface. The servant had already begun to go. I ran after him. Alexander stood outside the main door of the royal wing. Without a word, he took my hand and led me into the library.

'Ask me, instead of sneaking in here. I've told Lysimachus to be more watchful.'

'But will you show me everything?'

'Unlikely, but there's more than enough for you here, even with me present. Aren't the sunbeams lovely, falling through these square openings in the wall?'

The light was strong enough for us to make out motes settling on the innumerable papyrus scrolls on the shelves.

Alexander's attention was caught by a fly. He chased it with a scroll he'd grabbed from the nearest shelf. The fly landed right in front of me, on a bench. He crept towards the bench, raised the scroll and stared at the insect. The fly didn't move.

'Well, why don't you get it?' I asked impatiently.

'It's not the same fly, Phyllis.'

'May I see what's in the scroll you're holding?'

He didn't answer.

'You said I could look.'

He perused it quickly before handing it to me. It was headed 'Never'. The first lines were, 'Beaks that have never pecked', 'Feet that have never walked', 'Wings that have never flown', 'Teeth that have never bitten', 'Arms that have never embraced' and 'Fingers that have never wrapped themselves round a cup'.

I tried to read what was under each heading, but at that moment he grabbed the scroll.

'Can't you tell me what's written there?'

Hesitantly he unrolled the papyrus and read:

'The thoroughly good human being, and heroes, may be found in the Invisible Library in a large section called "Illusions", if not there, they may be in the section "Supposedly True Stories".'

He rolled up the scroll.

'Couldn't I read it?'

'Take the scrolls on that shelf,' he said pointing to the nearest wall.

I found scrolls with the following titles, 'Embarrassing Tales, Excluding Backbiting, Malicious Pleasure Section'. The material that followed was subdivided into, 'Philip, My Father', 'Antipater', 'Darius'. Other scrolls I saw before we had to leave, were 'Massive Exaggerations', 'Abortive Methods of Punish-ment and Execution' and 'Exaggerations Bordering on White Lies'. One of the biggest was a scroll he wouldn't let me open entitled 'Last Words of the Dying'. This was larger than the scrolls 'Man' and 'Woman'. Beneath 'Man' I managed to glimpse the subtitles 'Men's Hundred Routes to Destruc-tion', 'A Study of Men and the Death Wish', 'Why the Death Wish is More Prevalent in Men Than Women' and 'Things I've Done to Impress Men'. That was the last thing I was able to read before he led me out. By the door stood a large pot containing the charred remains of several scrolls.

'What were those, Alexander?'

'Bits of Persian history.'

'That would have made interesting reading, wouldn't it?'

'Possibly.'

'Why did you destroy them?'

'To humble the Persians. So that they wouldn't regain the self-esteem they once had. They need to feel they've been destroyed. To allow their historical sources to survive, well written as they certainly were, would be like blowing on the embers of the Persian Empire, which I have spent ten years and hundreds of thousands of lives in subjugating.'

A servant called to him, and Alexander went out into the hall. I saw my chance to grab the scroll entitled, 'A Study of Men and the Death Wish'. I unrolled it. It made me start when I saw that it was written in the first person:

I cannot stop,
rolling faster and faster towards annihilation.
Am I so brutal because I wish to meet my match,
A man both willing and able to kill me?
I'm rolling down a boulder-strewn slope that ends
    in scree.
As yet the speed wouldn't prevent me
from jumping out of the cart
if only Thanatos wasn't hugging me so hard.
The torch I carry is about to go out. Help me.

'Phyllis, are you coming?'
'Yes,' I called, put the scroll back and ran towards the voice.

I stood plucking thrushes, entrails in the bucket on my right, feathers to the left. A closed carriage arrived in the drill square, drawn by two horses. Dawn had just broken. The horizon was a greyish-black with a thin, red rim. One of the two riders swayed in the saddle. It looked as if he'd dozed off.

The day had begun so peacefully. Priamos let me and a couple of assistants stand outside because he was going to joint the birds. All I knew was that orders had been given about a guest who would be arriving from one of the Greek city states. The king had stated that thrush and mushrooms was this visitor's favourite dish, the other courses had been left to Priamos' discretion. The company was considered small, as there wouldn't be more than twenty-five at the meal, in addition to the guest of honour.

I asked Priamos if he knew who this guest was. He nodded. As he said no more, I decided to say no more myself. Alexander had told me I could depend on him. He certainly did. Priamos was from Byzantium, had been an officer, but had been wounded at the battle of Issus. He had a Persian wife and four children who lived in the camp outside the city walls. It would have been hard to find a more loyal man. Twice he'd been severely ill after tasting the king's food, but he never mentioned this to Alexander. He knew about us and had also, up to then, followed the king's orders: to act as if nothing had happened, even with me.

The night had been hot and close. After I'd removed every feather, Zara skinned the birds talking all the while about how she'd been taken prisoner by our army when she was tending sheep in Bactria. Priamos cut up the birds and steeped them in a marinade of oil, salt, mint and ice so that they wouldn't turn in the heat. Alexander ought to know that everything he said about Priamos was correct. Loyal to his king and kind to me.

The men who dismounted in the dusty drill square were grimy. They must have ridden all night. The riders opened the carriage door and spoke a name I couldn't catch. The man in the carriage was obviously sleeping deeply.

I went to tip the feathers and skin into a slop pail. Magpies and crows waited a short distance away, ready to descend on the remains as soon as I was out of sight. When I got back to my trestle, Zara was waiting for a new job. She gave little cause for complaint, but self-motivation wasn't her strong point. Even though she spoke no Greek, she should have known that the utensils needed washing immediately after use, without me having to point and mime. I was mulling this over when an elderly man with white hair and beard emerged from the carriage.

His hair was plastered to his high forehead. The crown of his head was shiny, but his beard was thick and curly. He

stepped down from the carriage with a certain amount of difficulty; not, I guessed because of his age, but because he'd just
woken up. He was wearing a white tunic, a buckle on his right
shoulder clasped the blue cape he wore over it. One rider held
out his arm to support him. He pushed it firmly aside. The
two horsemen positioned themselves behind him and awaited
orders. I noticed they were unarmed.

The three of them stayed where they were, the man with
white hair tugged at his cape and the buckle fell into the dust.
Instantly, one of the riders crouched down to pick up the orna-
ment, the other just prevented the cape from sharing the same
fate. After a while the man raised his right leg and stamped
his sandal in the sand so that a cloud of dust hid him for a
moment. He was tall, with a powerful face and body, I took
him to be about sixty.

I caught a sound, turned and found myself looking
straight into the green eyes of Priamos. He said, 'The only man
the conqueror of the world listens to.' I looked towards the
square again. The white-haired man was moving slowly in our
direction and mumbling. Priamos wiped his hands and just
before he went up to him he said:

'The wise man from Stagira, the king's counsellor and
teacher: Aristotle.'

The last night I shared a bed with Alexander, he was in a good
mood. He got up early and went to the table with the big gold

casket, and took out the scroll of the *Iliad*, with Aristotle's written comments.

'Does Aristotle mention the conundrum Achilles faced, either to remain at home and grow old, or to attack Troy?' I asked, pretending not to know the answer.

His eyes lit up for an instant. He was standing awkwardly, but found the quotation straight away. He read Aristotle's words aloud:

' "Achilles did the right thing by attacking Troy; it displayed his greatness and his invincibility. He chose eternal fame and an early death, rather than living a long life." Phyllis, such words, such words . . . '

'Well, what about them?'

'They've been my maxim.'

All the time I've known Alexander, every time he's arrived at a new place he's begun gathering any stones, plants, animals and birds which are new to him, and he's sent them home so that Aristotle could add further species to his vast collection. No service has been too small or too great when it came to his mentor.

No sooner had we set up camp in Ecbatana than Alexander brought together several dozen scholars, many of them chosen by Aristotle himself, and instructed them to pack the finds in crates that had several layers and compartments. As soon as this was done, the crates were dispatched by horse and cart to Aristotle in Athens. Alexander sent him presents, gold, precious stones, vases and furniture, especially divans, from his conquests, to show Aristotle his gratitude for everything he'd been taught. According to Priamos, the king has given Aristotle no less than three hundred and thirty talents quite recently. That's more than three years' pay for a general, as far as I know. Surely Aristotle must be one of the wealthiest men in Greece?

Now here he was, right in front of my eyes.

Aristotle spotted Alexander first. He turned his back on the king and pretended he didn't know he was there. Alexander placed himself in front of him, took his hand hesitantly, stroked his cheek. Aristotle turned away. Alexander ordered the horsemen to move off. I'd never seen Alexander in this position before, he was an inferior, and not just an ordinary servant but one who was anxious, fearful of doing the least thing amiss.

It was odd to see Aristotle, who was actually taller and more graceful than the king, playing the sulky child that Alexander clearly had to coax into the palace. Alexander tried grasping him affably above the elbow, once, twice. Aristotle told him to keep his distance. Alexander retreated a couple of steps before advancing again. Perhaps Aristotle didn't notice this. It seemed that Alexander interpreted his silence as a sign that they were once again on intimate terms. But when Alexander put his arm around him, Aristotle started and told his pupil off roundly.

They looked like a pair of mating birds. We kitchen staff wondered if the king would get his guest of honour indoors at all. Priamos didn't forbid us to watch, he was following developments himself. With a despairing gesture he said that the same thing had happened the last time Aristotle had come on a visit. Priamos believed that Aristotle had a long-standing disagreement with the king about introducing Persian customs and giving Persians important positions in the government. According to Priamos, Aristotle hadn't behaved like this since Alexander and his army had overrun Egypt. Aristotle believed it was pointless to hold on to this territory. The Egyptians were, in every sense, on a lower level than the Greeks. With his own ears Priamos had heard Aristotle shout after Alexander that non-Greeks were barbarians. Priamos disagrees with the philosopher. His wife is Persian and, he says, she's as knowledgeable as the Greek women he knows. My experience is different. Zara's nice enough, but what does she really know? I've got the feeling that she makes herself agreeable because she wants to fit in and feather her nest.

In the afternoon I learnt that Aristotle and Alexander were visiting military leaders. Lysimachus was ill. Having assured myself there was no one inside the royal apartments, I slipped in unnoticed. There were no sounds from behind the library door. As quietly as I could, I pushed the door open and stole inside.

I found the scroll I'd been reading a few days earlier when Alexander had interrupted me. It lay exactly where I'd put it down. I couldn't hear anyone outside. I searched with my finger until I found the place where the narrator, whom I took to be Alexander, was being embraced by Thanatos, the god of death:

I dearly wish I could have felt things like Sappho, and written,

> Just now the golden-sandaled Dawn
> Peered through the lattice of my room;
> Why must thou fare so soon, my Phaon?

I sit in the cart and roll down the stony hillside. The sky is on fire, my sword is my staff, my bow and arrow my lyre, Babylon is my swamp, the streets crack, the palace is a hovel of intrigue and everyone lusts for a piece of me. I lie in the throne room, starving wild dogs snap at my arms and legs, I cannot rise. Nobody lifts a finger. A circle of thousands stand and watch with faces like clenched fists.

I can't get out of the cart.

I own everything I see around me: mountains, cities, palaces, temples, soldiers, generals, admirals, the gold, the precious stones, all the men, women, wine, food, animals, actors, lyre players, north, south, east and west, but I can't manage to haul myself out of the cart.

The speed increases.

I avoid battle, I want to die undefeated, I've become so vain that I do not lead my soldiers into battle. I allow myself to be sidetracked by the lickspittles of the court, who have never known the front line, I betray my soldiers, my realm, my gods.

Soon I won't be able to breathe. The noise increases, the bumping becomes more violent, I see where things are heading, there's nothing to hold on to. The sky turns darker, the dust forces open my mouth, my whisper is a shout.

Further down it went on:

Hold your tongues.

The whole world will probably drown my melancholy with joy and cause each hair, nostril and the nails of my eyes to be buried.

Hold your tongues.

As soon as you witness my death
no matter where (*the next three words are impossible to decipher*).

A murderer might try to poison me
cut me down with dagger or sword.

Hold your tongues.

It's in vain. Save yourselves the effort.

I've got ten lives.

With each attempt I become myself once more.

Each time I die,

I die rejoicing,

standing.

Hold your tongues.

Cowards,

> I am Alexander,
> each time you murder me, my obstinate flame
> burns higher, I rise again and hammer
> thoughts of defeat into their skulls.

At the very bottom, I caught sight of these lines. He was clearly in a different mood when he wrote:

> A full moon over the Hindu Kush
> Forty-three towering, snowy peaks.
> The only thing that moved was the eagle's eye.

'You didn't fool me this time.'

Lysimachus stood in front of me. I looked straight into his thin, lantern-jawed face.

'You've no business here alone. It's my duty to report this to the king.'

If he said anything, I'd never get the chance to sneak in again. Security would be tightened and my insight into Alexander's hidden world would cease.

'What can I do to stop you speaking to him?'

'Nothing.'

I took his right hand and laid it on my left breast.

The following evening a servant entered my room without knocking. He stood in the doorway.

'I've been commanded to say: "Pick the flower."'

He looked embarrassed. The words signified that I should go at once to the king's chamber. 'Pay homage to the gods' meant that I should go to the temple as quickly as possible. The king could lie with whoever he wanted, at any time of the day or night, but he wasn't a fool. Even a great military leader is susceptible to gossip and rumour. It was apparent that he feared Roxane had found allies within the army.

I hurried up the broad back stairs to Alexander's room. I thought he wanted to speak to me about Aristotle. He stood waiting at the open door. He looked sombre.

'What was wrong with Aristotle?'

'Get undressed.'

I just stood there.

'Don't you understand what I'm saying?'

He began to kiss me, the kisses got more fervent, he said he didn't want to talk, he pulled off my clothes, pushed me back on to the bed. It seemed as if he were in a frenzy, he thrust into me. He finished.

'Bring me that wine over there.'

I got out of the great bed and fetched the flagon. I gathered my clothes and began to get dressed, I wanted to go back to my room.

'The king commands you to lie under the blanket, I'll tell you when you've got permission to leave the room.'

I lay down and pulled the blanket up to my chin.

'Over your head! You're not allowed to watch.'

I was relieved to see him smiling. I could hear him leaving the room. After a while he came back.

'Arise, nymph,' he said taking my hand.

Naked we entered the bathroom. The gold bath with room for two, one of the spoils from the Persian king, had been filled with hot water and aromatic oils. Rose petals floated on the water. He studied my body. I loved it. We got into the bath.

'You can say what you like about the Persians, but they certainly know how to make baths,' he said and flicked some water at me.

Suddenly he stood up.

'I forgot that I'm dining with General Medios. I promised to listen to his arguments against Nearchus' Arabian plans.'

'Weren't we going to be together?' I asked as he walked across the tiles, dripping.

'I'll be back sometime tonight.'

'You haven't told Priamos. How's he going to test the food and wine?'

'Don't worry about it.'

'What about Aristotle?' I said.

He pushed me down into the bath. I was scared he might drown me. I grasped the edge with both hands and got my head above water.

'Are you going to drink yourself to death, Alexander?'

'D'you know what you are, Phyllis?'

He considered for a moment.

'You're a fly in the horse's mane, an insect clinging on for a cheap ride.'

Next morning I saw Alexander in the servants' wing. He was emerging on all fours from his dresser's room, he was naked. When the dresser ventured to mention that he ought to wear 'something or other', Alexander hit out at him and called for more to drink.

In the evening he fetched me from my room and steered me to the king's apartments. I took his hand.

'Do you remember the first time we met?' I asked.

'No.'

'I was serving you and the other soldiers in the mess tent. A short way from Ecbatana.'

He looked at me doubtfully.

'You were disguised as a common soldier, to find out who was working against you.'

'Are you joking?'

'Where did you think we met?'

He thought about it.

'Here.'

'Where here?'

'By the Euphrates.'

'There are several cities on the Euphrates.'

'What right have you to interrogate me?'

'I'm not interrogating you. We're in Babylon.'

'Yes, I do know that.'

'Have you seen me before this evening?'

'Don't be impertinent.'

'But why am I here with you?'

It didn't seem as if he was paying attention to what I said. He disappeared for an instant and returned with a flagon and two cups. He poured the wine, downed his own cup and replenished it.

'Is there something about me you—'

I hesitated, as if I were afraid of the answer.

'—like?'

'Like?'

'Something you're fond of?'

'There certainly is.'

'And that is?'

'You're a good talker.'

'What's my name?'

'I know that.'

'And my name is?'

'Penelope. Can you ask Olympias to come?'

'Your mother isn't in Babylon,' I said, and went to my room at the other end of the palace.

I couldn't sleep. I was afraid to leave him on his own. I went back. No one was standing guard outside his apartments. I heard his voice beyond the door. I pushed it open.

The shadows from the torches danced on the wall behind Alexander. He stood in the middle of the floor rambling incoherently. I managed to make out words like 'Antipater', 'strangled' and 'can't take any more'. His voice alternated between fear and anger. He could find no way out of the tangle of thoughts in which he'd enmeshed himself during the night, even though day was breaking. His gaze was far away. I was a stranger. I placed my hands over his large, cold ones. I grasped his fingers.

'Alexander,' I shouted. 'I'm here. Can you hear me?'

I squeezed his hands several times, but felt no reaction.

Suddenly, and for some reason unbeknown to me, he drew my hands towards him and said tenderly:

'Just imagine, some people think of women as objects. That's such an underestimation of you. You're like straw.'

All at once a playfulness came into his eyes, like a cat that carries a mouse in its jaws, its teeth pressing lightly on its prey.

'You catch fire so quickly.'

It was good to see him smile again. I reached for the cup on the table in front of him. The wine warmed my stomach, my legs grew unsteady. My head became lighter and balanced more and more loosely on my body. I was starting to get drunk.

'D'you know what we are?' I said.

His silence didn't hold me back.

'We're two cripples. I'm lame on my left side, you on your right. If we were tied together, what would we look like?'

'A sea turtle,' he answered glibly.

'Nobody must be allowed to roll us on our back, you hear?'

I grasped his shoulders and shook him.

'If the two of us were bound together, Phyllis, we'd sink faster than a millstone,' he said in a low voice.

Aristotle was absent from the next three meals. When at last he returned to the table, I was in the kitchen chopping mushrooms for the side dish. Priamos was serving. It wasn't long before he came up and stood next to me, shaking his head and sighing heavily.

'Do you know what the king came out with? He said he was overjoyed to see his teacher again. He apologized for his behaviour towards Aristotle, and then ordered all the finest dishes to be placed in front of the philosopher. Talk about humbling yourself. Aristotle said he was horrified by Alexander's inability to understand that Persians were second-class people.'

'And the king retaliated?' I enquired.

'He reminded Aristotle that he was the one who'd always taught his pupil to search for the golden mean, and that it had to be possible to select the best from Greek, Persian and Babylonian culture. Aristotle jumped up from his divan, tore off his napkin and marched angrily out.'

That same evening I got into the dress that Alexander said I looked best in. It was long and dark green. I wore my amber necklace, and I put on the gold bracelet he'd given me with its Babylonian winged lion. I was ready long before I was due to meet him. I'd been looking forward to it for several days. We might even talk at last about the philosopher's behaviour when he arrived at the palace, I thought as I finished applying my make-up in my room.

There was a knock at the door. A page told me 'to accompany him to the king'.

'Did the king say nothing else?' I asked.

'You heard what I said.'

Even though the young man's tone was frosty, I didn't feel uneasy.

He preceded me into the audience chamber, and then the anxiousness came. I saw Alexander straight away in silhouette, the light fell differently on the man beside him. Alexander stood in front of his gold and ivory throne that was shaped like a peacock's display, five amphorae formed a circle around the men. Flowers filled the chamber. It was easy to recognize the white hair and curly beard of Aristotle. Alexander looked grave. I couldn't utter a word, I was breathing hard, there was a thudding in my head. I stood as if at attention. Why couldn't we be alone? I took a step nearer, in order to see Alexander's eyes better. I thought that if we looked into one another's eyes, he would turn back into himself again. He tried to look away.

Aristotle spoke first. He talked slowly, without moving his hands.

'When you stand before King Alexander, you will address him as "Your Highness",' he said, staring at me.

I didn't speak.

'Perhaps Your Highness wishes to say something?' said Aristotle.

After many disjointed words, Alexander said:

'You can keep your job. I'll talk to Priamos. We won't meet alone again. You're a bad influence on me.'

'Did you hear the king's words?' Aristotle asked, turning to me. 'This is a generous offer on his part. It's for Macedonia's good, and your own.'

I noticed that Aristotle was studying me. I glanced towards him. I smiled. I was scared.

I continued to say nothing, Aristotle summoned the page who'd conducted me to the chamber. He was told to take me back to my room. I didn't look at Alexander as I was escorted out. Now they're going to kill me, I thought.

Back in my own room I imagined the guards coming for me at any moment. I tried the door several times, unlocked it and looked out into the passage. All was quiet. The following day I went to work. Priamos and the others behaved quite normally.

That reassured me a little. Priamos asked me to buy some special black olives at one of the smaller markets in a part of the city I'd never been to before. I sprinted out through the open city gate, walked through the barracks area, until I arrived at the market and obtained two pails of the much-prized olives. Eventually I found my way back. Not long after, I became aware of the stink of war. The stink of dead horses and the piss-sodden, hard-tramped ground. A defeated army lay spread across the flat and once-fertile fields before me. It wasn't just the smoke from the fires but the stench of people and of war that reached me. It was too late to turn back. I saw an officer from Thrace whom I recognized. A friend of my husband's.

'Who are these people?' I asked.

I suspected they were allies because the men hadn't been executed and were allowed so close to Babylon. I felt uneasy as soon as I'd finished my question.

'An army from Lydia.'

'Lydia?' I repeated.

I don't know whether he noticed that my eyes became moist.

'Who were they fighting?'

'I haven't a clue.'

He nodded towards the dying men. 'They haven't a clue, either. I've asked them. What a pathetic army,' he said, sighing. 'And just think, Phyllis, they were supposed to be of some help.'

He drew in his breath, 'Some help.'

I left without a goodbye, I didn't want him to see my tears and start asking questions.

They were our allies, but separated from our soldiers. There were several hundred, maybe a thousand men. They were on land that looked as if it had grown corn. Now they lay exhausted, dying or dead, blue, white, grey, yellow bodies between the fires. A few tattered tents had been erected. The dead had been stacked in piles; I counted four, there were others but I didn't want to look at them. Several, who still lived among the piles of corpses, huddled together in groups. In their death agonies some of them called out for their mothers, and sought protection under other bodies. A gust of wind caused the smoke from the fires to lift. The ground all the way to the Euphrates was covered with dead and seriously wounded men and horses.

The living made the camp look like a moving carpet. The air was filled with plaintive sounds that rose and fell, but never ceased. Although it was less than a year since I'd been in the war, it felt like an eternity. I'd led a sheltered life in this beautiful city while the moaning, screaming and crying had continued outside its walls. Pilferers from Babylon moved about stealing weapons, clothes and jewellery from the dying who couldn't defend themselves. A few of the dead were stripped, item by item, with the greatest care. Nobody reacted. Some of the corpses were so rigid that it was difficult to remove the clothes without ruining them. The only people who shouted were the officers who tried to chase the robbers away. Sooty ravens perched on the roofs of the nearest houses, waiting for a chance to hack into the dead horses whose taut hide covered their bloated bellies.

Those who lay there had fought our wars. The sight reminded me of the life I'd left behind, where you saw soldiers or others who followed the army—people you'd got to know, perhaps even become fond of—getting badly wounded or killed. How many times had I hoped that the stomachs of dying friends and acquaintances would quickly fill with blood, so that their throats would turn pale, their eyes glaze over and their bodies stiffen.

The men who lay all around me should have known that it was I who'd persuaded Alexander to bring Lydia into the war. I even remember what we talked about late that night, after I'd got my way:

'Can't you come to bed?' I asked.

'More people die in bed than anywhere else.'

Finally he lay down.

'How did your father die?' he asked.

'An arrow. As he was fetching a loaf of bread. He and the other men were mad with hunger.'

'What happened to the loaf?'

'He gave it the nearest man before he fell.'

'Soldiers should have a sense of honour.'

'What a pretentious word. Why don't you fight any more?' I asked. 'War is where you won your reputation. You don't belong in this palace. Without you on the battlefield, your soldiers' future is merely to enrich the soil of a land they scarcely know the name of.'

I didn't expect an answer. I've never been able to hate Alexander sufficiently to wish him the death his soldiers die, with an arrow in the eye or face down in the mud. A friend of my husband's, an officer, was left lying on the field after the battle of Issus. The army pushed forward. The medical corps hadn't found him. I was the first to notice him. He looked straight at me, his guts spilling out. Blood welling from his mouth.

'What can I do?' I shouted. He tried to say something, but his words drowned in blood. I bent over him. He swallowed.

'Kill me,' he said.

I blame myself for not being able to grant his final wish. I loathe my own cowardice. I have no reason to accuse Alexander or anyone else. The soldier had fought for something he believed in, the thing that Alexander had inculcated in us: To conquer the world. He met his death with dignity, but I could have spared him great suffering. The king these soldiers fought and gave their lives for, is ignorant of the armies and men dying on the outskirts of his new metropolis.

The week before Hephaestion died, the army and all the rest of us had marched for seven days to Ecbatana. What occurred the day after our arrival, caused me and others to wonder if the king was losing his wits, or perhaps worse still: creating situations in which people would become so incensed that they'd want to murder him. In the course of the feast hosted by Atropates, the Satrap of Media, Hephaestion told us servers how proud he was of his new title. Alexander had made him chiliarch. Most of the generals felt themselves sidelined. Alexander was seated on his throne. Hephaestion sat on a throne next to him. Officials from all across the Persian plateau approached the royal throne and fell to their knees. Alexander dismissed the well-wishers. An elderly man asked Hephaestion in Greek if he had saluted the king inappropriately. Hephaestion shrugged his shoulders. He and Alexander sat drinking from large silver cups while they were addressed in words, the majority of which they found incomprehensible. Large quantities of wine appeared. The pair became more and more intoxicated.

Gifts presented to Alexander were opened in front of him by two servants. Gifts which couldn't be drunk, he waved away.

Competitions in sprinting, discus, wrestling, poetry and lyre-playing in honour of Dionysus took place in front of the king without his paying any heed to them. Nor would he greet the actors and singers who'd been summoned from every corner of Greece, even though they were his hand-picked favourites.

I implored the king's cup-bearer to pour away some of the wine or to 'forget' a few of his demands. Hephaestion fell off his throne in the act of ordering more drink. The satrap told the cup-bearer that the king would be incensed if they didn't get what they asked for. Hephaestion ended up lying next to the king's throne. Alexander laughed. Water was sprinkled over Hephaestion, he didn't react. Alexander continued drinking. I begged a couple of the bodyguards to carry Hephaestion to the court physician, Glaucion. Alexander noticed that Hephaestion was being lifted.

'Don't disturb Glaucion now. He'll only want to make me drink less. It's our duty to pay homage to Dionysus,' he bellowed.

Alexander fell asleep. Glaucion was summoned. He told two of Hephaestion's servants to carry him to the palace which was close by. When the king awoke, he was told that Hephaestion had gone to bed. Alexander shrugged and left for the games with Atropates instead. I found out what happened next from one of Alexander's bodyguards, whose name I've sworn to keep secret. Glaucion went to the palace where Hephaestion was lying, to instruct the servants to make sure that if he woke, he wasn't to start drinking again. After

Glaucion had received their assurances, he left for the theatre to watch Sophocles' *Electra*.

Hephaestion came to while Glaucion was at the theatre, and immediately demanded some boiled chicken. In an unattended moment he got hold of a flagon of wine from under the bed, which he'd concealed the previous evening. By the time Glaucion was called, Hephaestion was dead. Glaucion said that his heart couldn't take any more.

Alexander came at the gallop. Someone, identity unknown, had told him what had happened. He was weeping as he jumped off his horse and ran to the bed where Hephaestion lay. Alexander started shaking him, wailing and lamenting. He shouted to all those around him that nobody had meant so much to him. He cried out that Hephaestion was the only person who'd loved him, not because he was a king, but for himself as a human being.

The king's sorrow and pain were genuine. But no less than mine, after being betrayed by Alexander. The anger and misery I feel, resembles Alexander's after the death of Hephaestion.

The sun had risen twenty-six times before Alexander spoke a word to me. I'd seen him many times, but I was invisible, a cook who could have been anyone. Seeing his agony was infinitely worse than witnessing how much he must have loved Hephaestion. I'd become a part of him. I felt his suffering in my body, in my voice and in my head.

Alexander fasted for three days, declared national mourning in Asia, prohibited music and singing in military camps and gave orders that the manes of all army horses and asses should be shorn. His orders for destroying the god of healing's temple in Ecbatana were not merely foolish but insane, and had more to do with wine in the blood than his having been seized with divine power. On the second day of fasting, he sent a messenger to Amon's oracle at Siwa asking if, from now on, it would be permissible to make sacrifices to Hephaestion as a god. Alexander received an emphatic no from the high priest. The worship of Hephaestion as a hero was quite enough, even though nobody knew which deed had qualified him for that distinction, he declared.

Alexander likened himself to Achilles. He even said that his sorrow was similar to that Achilles felt when he lost his finest soldier, Patroclus. Alexander cut off his hair just as

Achilles had done when his best soldier fell in battle. It was a disconcerting comparison. Hephaestion had not died like a hero. He'd drunk himself to death. The king gave orders that no one should be appointed chiliarch to the Companion Cavalry after Hephaestion. He decreed that from then on the section was to be called 'Hephaestion's Regiment' and when on the move, his portrait was to be carried in front of the men.

Alexander decided that Hephaestion's remains would be taken to Babylon, where his favourite architect, Dinocrates, would design the world's largest funerary monument, and a shrine to Hephaestion would be erected in Egypt.

The world has never seen a bigger funeral pyre, five storeys and sixty-five metres high. Those of us who worked for the army were drawn up by trade. We cooks and servers stood next to the rope-makers and smiths. The base of the pyre was square, each side measuring two hundred metres. Beautiful sculptures looked out from every storey: on one floor I recall gilded centaurs, on another bulls and lions, on a third Macedonian and Persian arms. At the very top stood sirens, gilded and silvered, behind turquoise and crimson veils. After the pyre had burnt out, it looked as if the army had razed a village. The following day Glaucion was brought before Alexander in the square, where the two thrones still stood. The doctor was barely able to walk, his toes had been broken by one of the king's bodyguards.

'No architect can erect a monument, however large, that can reflect the enormity of the pain I feel. A monument would be an insult to my sorrow, a pale reflection of my loss at Hephaestion's death,' Alexander roared at Glaucion. 'You shall be crucified.'

'I tried to save him,' Glaucion bleated in despair, before being dragged off.

I went to the crucifixion at dawn the next day. I'd never seen a crucifixion before. The square was full. When Glaucion arrived surrounded by eight soldiers, the public was moved back to the edges of the square and the surrounding streets. Some people threw stones and rotten fruit at Glaucion. The soldiers shouted that the crowd had to move away to allow the two soldiers who were carrying the cross, to lay it down so that they could begin to nail the doctor to it. Glaucion struggled when they tried to nail him. It took a blow to the head from a stone to keep him quiet. Two of the soldiers quickly nailed his hands. By the time he came to, he was hanging at head height above the dusty square. The soldiers stationed themselves on the perimeter of the crowd. We ran towards the cross. We looked up at him. The soldiers wouldn't allow anyone to throw stones. I wanted to go, I couldn't tear myself away. A sound came from up above. A weak, plaintive sound. It was the stifled sound that rises up from the depths of the soul when it's over-whelmed with fear. I have known it in my own breast. Glaucion's tortured voice evoked an anxiety within me that I couldn't fathom. Again I tried to leave, without success. Behind the figure of Glaucion the daylight waxed relentlessly.

Two days later, when the smoke from Hephaestion's pyre had ceased, the army massacred the Cossaeans, who raised tolls on travellers in the Zagros Mountains between Babylon and Ecbatana. Alexander took it out on a mountain people, and called the massacre of children and adults a 'propitiatory sacrifice to the spirit of the dead man'.

I don't blame Alexander for avenging himself. Had I been able to, I'd have put both him and Aristotle in the audience chamber with their feet in mortar and let the roof and walls fall on top of them, before setting fire to the whole thing.

I'm no monarch with unlimited power but my revenge, I pondered as I watched Priamos standing outside the kitchens cleaning cabbages and turnips, would be as great as the love I'd once felt. Provided I didn't say anything, or show how great my anger was, I had the chance to take my victim by surprise.

When Alexander came to our final tryst in the temple, prior to Aristotle's visit, he was unsteady and jovial.

'The night about us is too deep,' he said, 'I've only been drunk once, but that one time lasted more than a year. I don't always drink, Phyllis. I've got to sleep as well. In the morning I'll be sober.'

Trying to make Alexander stop drinking was about as hard as trying to lasso a lightning bolt.

It's such a short time since he kindled my obsession, since he made me drop everything. I picture the way we lie entwined, my thigh touching his, his chest against my back, I flex my ankle slightly, he wakes, his fingers rest on my shoulders before his hand moves to clasp my breast gently, the rough pad of his thumb caressing my nipple. I've thought of us holding a small child by the hand. Yes, I've thought of him as the father of our child. He lets his hand wander over my hip. He's searching for the way in, I open my legs.

It was an easy matter to ask the servant who had escorted me to the audience chamber, to help me meet Aristotle. The servant was to explain to the philosopher that I had to see him alone, because I'd got something he'd left behind the last time we'd met. The youth didn't ask a single question, he just stood there in front of me. It made me uneasy.

'The king won't like it if you refuse,' I said.

With that he left.

I was playing for high stakes. It was something I'd learnt from Alexander.

Naturally I was nervous, but the knowledge that I'd never forgive myself if I didn't try, was stronger. I stood behind my door waiting, listening to see if Aristotle had sent the guards to arrest me. That was one possibility, the other was that he might come with Alexander, or that the servant would return and say that Aristotle wouldn't come.

After a while I heard footsteps outside the door, the familiar sigh of sandals on marble. There was a cautious knock. I waited a moment before answering. I'd managed to get into the dress Aristotle had seen me in the last time we'd met. I smiled as I opened the door and asked him in. He glanced about before crossing the threshold. His neck and ears were flushed. His hair and beard had been combed. His beard had also been trimmed. He went over to the hole in the wall, and said that the view surprised him.

'I've just been speaking to the king. I told him that Babylon cannot be the capital of the kingdom. Every Greek would be incensed.'

I noticed my hands were trembling.

'But why are you telling me this?' I asked.

'Because you've had influence with him.'

'I've always disagreed with the king.'

'That's not what I've heard.'

'These people here in Babylon are barbarians. Their customs, religion, language and culture demonstrate that they're much more primitive than us.'

He nodded. I realized I was feeling calmer. He turned slowly towards me. I could see some beads of sweat high on his brow. I said:

'The architectural style of this city is hopeless. The Babylonians haven't produced a single work of artistic or literary merit.'

'You're not just beautiful, you're intelligent as well,' he said.

'Aren't you being a bit generous with your compliments? Isn't that because we share so many points of view?'

He shook his head and came a step closer.

'You really are . . . exceptional,' he said.

My arms hung limply.

'Alexander's told me that you've done some reading. Tell me what you've read, and I'll tell you who you are.'

'Plato, Herodotus, Thucydides . . .'

'Lies,' he mumbled.

'What d'you mean?'

'You realize I saved your life?'

'When?' I queried.

'The king wanted you put to death, but the queen and I appreciate that you have certain qualities.'

'The last time I met you, you refused to let me see the king any more. Was it Roxane who asked you to come to Babylon and get me out of the way?'

'Keep away from him. It's for your own good. Be grateful you're still alive.'

A mild breeze wafted in. I recognized the scent of the maples as I looked into those grey eyes and felt the fear rise within me.

'Aren't you going to say anything? Don't you know that willpower in the weak is called obstinacy? There are those who believe it adds to the character. Surely, you're not one of them, are you, Phyllis?'

He smiled, it smoothed out his wrinkles.

'We're fortunate, we live in the best of all worlds,' I managed to say at last.

'I fear you're right.'

He peered out and continued:

'Do you often drink with him?'

I didn't know what he was hinting at. I bent down and adjusted one of my sandals.

'Some believe in gods, but not in their own common sense. Nor have they any cause to,' he said.

'You're good-looking,' I said.

'Be truthful, Phyllis, admit you're lying.'

I felt myself blushing.

'Surely you wouldn't disagree that, at the very least, this haggard face could do with a little sleep?'

I tried to smile.

'Besides, I brought along a flagon of wine with a fine, distinctive taste, and two cups which I left out in the passage. Shall we each drink a cup?'

'That's kind of you, but it's not convenient at the moment. You haven't asked what it was you left behind,' I said trying to smile. 'That was your reason for coming, wasn't it?'

'Certainly.'

'It was just something I made up so that I could see you again.'

'Really?' he said.

'You saved me from the king,' I said. 'Thank you.'

'Did you invite me here so that you could thank me?'

'Yes.'

His eyes wandered around the room, and alighted on the narrow bunk.

'I'm a widower.'

He put a hand on my shoulder. I clasped the hairy wrist and lifted it off. He didn't resist.

'You deserve a better place than this,' I said.

He watched me curiously. I raised his hand and held it against my throat.

'Trust me,' I said. 'Alexander and I used a unique place for our assignations. You can enjoy it, too. No one will discover us there. I must go to work now, but I have a suggestion.'

I bent towards his ear and whispered a time and place.

'Are we agreed?' he asked.

'Yes,' I said.

He nodded and left without closing the door behind him. I shut the door, leant my back against it and tried to breathe calmly. There was a thudding at my temples. After a while I opened the door again. No one was in sight.

My mind encompasses everything I am, everything I have, and everything I want to be. It is bigger than this tiny room I sit, or lie in. It's not just a consoling but a pleasurable fact that those who've held me prisoner can't take my thoughts away from me. Nearly everything has gone, but no one will be able to make off with my thoughts as long as I live. You won't get hold of my dreams, either. I'm glad that Alexander hasn't even got a cell to walk about in, but must lie and be stared at the whole time by people who wish him no good.

A moment ago I fell asleep with my head on the table. I dreamt of dolphins and that I was riding on their backs. Ever since I was a small child I've heard about them. Father had once seen dolphins off the coast, not far from the Peloponnese. He drew and described them vividly to us children. It was after the battle of Issus that I saw my first dolphin. At the start of the battle everything went to plan. I, and many like me, felt certain of victory. I was intoxicated, but then quite suddenly the Persians advanced and spread panic in our ranks. I got separated from the other camp followers. Nearly a hundred of us were in the same desperate situation. The Persians killed half our number with their swords. Instead of shouting for help, which I knew was useless, I took to my heels.

I ran and ran until I came to the sea, I waded out into the turquoise breakers, determined to drown rather than let the enemy catch me. The waves slapped against my thighs. I ran on until I felt the way the current was trying to drag me with it, down into the depths, and carry me far away. I felt something smooth against my skin, I screamed, how I screamed. I thought for a moment it was a shark. Father had told me that sharks eat people. When I saw its head and its beaklike mouth, I knew it was a dolphin. It swam away from me a bit when it realized how scared I was. I recognized my father's description. I became calmer, it swam closer. At last it was so close that I could touch it. Its skin wasn't at all rough, as I'd anticipated, but smooth, grey and white. It swam under me, next to me, in front, and even jumped over me, as if it had changed into a bird. Father had never said anything about that, or was this one quite special? One thing he was right about was that it had its own distinctive smile, a friendly smile. Who are they? Have they taken part in our battles? Are they dead soldiers, or sibyls, or were they here before us? Are they laughing at us?

When I came to myself, I was lying on the beach listening to an outlandish noise that wasn't the sound of the waves, but something that only snails' shells, and every other whorled shell can produce, after the sound has revolved a few times in their hollow spirals. At first it was a moaning and hissing, then it turned into singing, then into buzzing, and finally it fell completely silent and the sun rose in the sky. I got up and began to walk inland. Hunger gnawed at me evermore relentlessly, I stumbled, I couldn't be bothered to get up. I propped my head on my elbows and ate clover which grew around me in profusion. I ate insects: flies, centipedes, some large ladybirds and mosquitoes. I also found some beetles I'd never seen before in the grass, vibrantly coloured. They were masters of disguise and had small shields over their innumerable thin, black legs which, to my surprise, they often managed to control as they crossed the ants' roads before I ate them.

My hand sought grass, toadstools that smelt nasty but tasted good, hairy, green leaves that sweated and crumpled up as I munched them. When a scorpion appeared, I screamed, without disturbing the creature's journey to the right and away. My cries were so loud that some of our soldiers heard me and brought me to safety.

On the day of my evening assignation with Aristotle, I'd asked the king's most trusted page to tell Alexander that I 'hoped to meet him at the usual time and place, and that I had something startling to offer him'. The page, who'd helped us arrange our meetings several times before, clearly hadn't heard anything about my fall from favour. On the contrary, he met me with confidence and smiled mischievously when I produced the word *startling*.

Aristotle met me at the appointed time. He was still a bit too fragrant. When perfume is splashed on, it becomes too heady, too sweet. I registered that he was unaccompanied. He greeted me formally and immediately wanted 'to see the couch where the king lay with you', as he expressed it.

The strange thing was that instead of feeling anxious and afraid, I was actually elated. I imagine Alexander must have had much the same feeling immediately before battles in which his army was outnumbered and the enemy knew the lie of the land better than he did. The thought of starting out as the underdog, gave me extra strength. I wasn't frightened of losing. I had everything to gain. That, at least, was what I told myself. After Aristotle had looked around and dwelt on the lovely, gold, four-branched oil lamp that Alexander had placed there, he went over to the bed.

'Take your clothes off,' he said.

'I will, but first of all I want to show you the veil dance that Alexander likes so much.'

He removed his clothes.

I danced round in a circle and pirouetted with my arms out, clutching the golden veil I'd got from Alexander in one hand. Aristotle was soon in bed. I stopped, went over to him, took his hand and drew his pale, elderly body replete with white chest and pubic hair, out on to the floor. We held hands and capered around each other several times.

'In a moment you'll feel something you've never experienced before.'

As I talked, his penis grew, until its reddish-blue tip pointed. He tried to hold me around the waist, I pushed his arm away.

'Down on all fours first.'

With some difficulty he obeyed my command. It was obvious this was something he hadn't done that often. His eyes were expectant, his face flushed. I noticed his skinny torso and hips.

When he was on his hands and knees, I began singing amorous words and seated myself on his bony back, while clasping his lean shoulders.

I heard footsteps outside. I sang louder. Aristotle was stronger than I'd imagined, but I took some of the weight on my feet so as not to dampen his lust. I threw the veil over his shoulders the moment before the door opened.

It's possible some will feel abhorrence at my words about Alexander's teacher, but I can assure them that I've tried to describe the situation as accurately as I can. To others it won't matter what I say. They won't believe me anyway.

The first to speak was Aristotle:

'Whore.'

Alexander contemplated Aristotle long enough for there to be no doubt that it was indeed the philosopher he was staring at. My former lover's horrified look was the best revenge I could have.

'Do you need some clothes?' Alexander asked him.

I didn't hear the answer, but got off and went past Alexander and the guards, out into the street and into the press of people, without a backward glance. I must have been more scared than I remember.

Although no one was in pursuit, I began to hurry across the puddles back to the palace. The evening rain had turned the ground to mud. I noticed a frog at my feet, its green and black skin, its beautiful limbs like fingers in a glove, eyes moving beneath their lids, throat puffing up as it gasped for air through its trembling mouth. In three leaps it cleared the pond.

I wanted to get to my room and change and go to the kitchens, even though I wasn't on duty. The kitchens were like an island in the palace. Everyone who worked there did their best and concentrated on their tasks. Priamos wasn't at work. Nobody said anything about the extra duty I was doing, those who did notice probably thought it was an arrangement between Priamos and me.

I was given fish to clean. The flesh was red and oily. Each one was no bigger than my hand. I concentrated on getting all the bones out of the fish and keeping ominous thoughts at bay.

I said goodnight to the staff still in the kitchens, took off my apron and went outside. The weather was dry and it was quiet, no light came from the royal wing. I knew that Alexander was at the admiral's home. I considered sneaking in at Nearchus', shouting out the tale of what Aristotle and I had got up to in the temple, and how Alexander had witnessed it. I walked down the slope from the kitchens to the bank of the Euphrates, to where the reeds were thickest. The river was fuller than usual after three weeks of rain. It was a long way to the other side. I knew that the Euphrates was at its deepest right in front of me. If I walked straight out between the tall, stiff reeds, no one would be able to see me. I glanced up at the night sky. I stared up, I turned dizzy. The stars were sharp and clear. My body was drawn towards the river, but my head felt the pull of the stars and the moon. I'd often considered life to be a gift but not any more. I thought how quickly the current would carry me away.

I caught the scent of some nearby roses. It reminded me that the roses would be standing on the bank when daylight returned: I wanted to see them again, and—I wanted to see Alexander one last time.

❧

Ski jumping was my life. The doctor had forbidden me to try any more jumps. It would be extremely risky. My ambition to jump at Holmenkollen was fast becoming a lost opportunity. I hadn't told my parents that I was ill. It was March, the last training day at Holmenkollen. Next season I'd be in even poorer shape. I was a couple of years too young to be allowed to jump from the world's most famous slope which towers high above Oslo. Every day I'd been able to see it from various angles.

It was now or never. I, who'd spent years training to pitch my body forward from the takeoff point and begin the curve of the jump, was about to lose everything. My skis were heavier than I remembered. I got up to the top. I placed my skies in the piste. There was almost no wind, but just enough motion in the air for a long jump. I'd never taken off from such a long slope. The wind became stronger. I clipped on my skis and glanced down the ramp. Crouching, I adjusted my goggles one last time. I felt giddy. Vague thoughts of derring-do and death coursed through my mind.

It was my turn. I talked to myself. I told myself out loud that I might kill myself. My legs weren't strong enough to take the landing. I repeated the words in the gust of wind. But first I wanted to fly, I didn't want to be a victim, to be patted, pitied, stuck in a wheelchair. I didn't want to land, I wanted to fly for the rest of my life, I shouted. The edge of the jump was a black, bottomless hole, with no end.

I longed to be there.

I was sitting on a horse, I pressed my heels into its flanks and made to ride in that direction.

I grabbed the handrail and pushed off.

The moon was large and full. It was a great help. On the slope I could hear the sound of the Euphrates. Down on the bank I hadn't noticed it. I didn't like walking in the evening darkness. When I heard noises a little way off, I hunted in the pocket of my tunic for the long nail I use in the kitchens to test if cakes are cooked through. When I return home in the evenings I always make sure to have it with me in case I'm attacked. Reaching the top of the incline I made up my mind to head to Admiral Nearchus' house. I saw lights from the palace. To get to where Alexander was, I had to follow an unlit path. I was almost there when I heard screams and shouts. I saw Alexander in the lead, then Nearchus, who fell down the stairs, behind these two came fifteen or sixteen men and three women.

I hid behind the hedge.

Of these, the first person I recognized was you, Antipater, and your son Cassander. Hasn't he been made a general now? You were walking side by side. I would have known Aristotle immediately, but he wasn't there. Aristotle had probably left already, I thought. Just then, in the darkness, I was looking forward to telling you and the other men what had happened. And if anyone was bold enough to tell me I was lying, I'd divulge that Aristotle had a large, reddish-brown birthmark, with two smaller ones below it. I would yell out all this as the guards closed in on me.

Medios was there as well. He brought up the rear saying that there was more than enough to drink at his house. It looked as if he was the soberest of the group. I checked for Priamos, who was usually present at every meal. He wasn't there. Roxane was absent too.

The women in the party weren't prostitutes, but serving women who were struggling to carry flagons of wine and baskets of food. The moon hung right above the large house and cast long shadows across the raucous company.

You and your son supported the king between you. Alexander was the most paralytic of all; him and Nearchus.

His tunic had slipped off his right shoulder, but Alexander didn't seem to care. He was sweating, his brow glistened. I could hear Medios saying that he'd go on ahead to wake the servants and warn them that company was expected. You were standing right by me, on the other side of the hedge.

'There's one way to find out if the king's lying,' Cassander said.

'How's that?' you asked.

'See if his lips move,' said Cassander.

'The king's not lying now,' you said.

You were holding Alexander up between you. Several times it looked like you were about to drop him. Just before he'd hit the ground, you'd managed to haul him up again. I could hear his snores. One of you said it was a good thing Aristotle wasn't there, it would have 'put a damper on the party'. When I could no longer see you, I got up warily. Suddenly, I felt a hand over my mouth, and I was thrown to the ground. Lying on my back in the grass I managed to reach into my pocket.

The voice above me had hardly managed to announce that he was part of the king's security, before I plunged the nail into him as far as it would go, just above where I assumed his navel lay. He bent over, as if he was indisposed and wanted to throw up. He just sat there, doubled up.

You were all still talking loudly. When I saw who I'd stabbed with my nail, I started. He raised his right arm as if to strike. The movement was only half completed when his arm sank. He managed nothing more.

I pulled the nail out, pressed it in where I thought his heart was. He twitched a couple of times. A cloud slid in front of the moon. I'd killed Alexander's servant. I wiped the nail on the tall, dry bulrush next to me.

The man on the ground had never done me any harm. I replaced the nail in my pocket.

Suddenly I remembered where I'd seen the three women before, the ones in the party that I could no longer hear. They helped the servers arrange food on platters and clear away after meals in the banquet hall at the palace. They'd seen me on several occasions, but the others, apart from Alexander and

Nearchus, wouldn't know me. I, on the other hand, recognized most of them from Alexander's descriptions. I managed to drag the dead man under some bushes. I was surprised how easy I found moving the body. Perhaps carrying and jointing animal carcases in the kitchens over the past few months had made me strong. I began to walk, forcing myself to move calmly at first, up the path and the steps after the others.

My stride quickened steadily. I love you, I hate you, Alexander, I muttered. I took the final flight of steps in two long strides. I'd make a scene and tell the company everything I'd been subjected to at the hands of Alexander and Aristotle. Loud and clear! I wasn't worried about the consequences, provided I could see the shame in Alexander's eyes. Two tall soldiers were stationed at the entrance, armed with swords.

'The king's head cook, Priamos, has ordered me to help with the serving.'

They nodded to one another. The front door was opened by one of the women, who told me to wait in the vestibule.

I had time to gaze around. There was a courtyard with a pool in the middle. From the vestibule a wide staircase led upward, to what I assumed were bedrooms. The house was of sand-coloured masonry. Its lines were straight. Within the courtyard, in front of the house, palm trees stood swaying in the night breeze. The ceilings were vaulted and white, and unencumbered by any sort of decoration. I recalled Alexander saying that Medios' villa was 'a pearl of Persian architecture, which the owner thinks is Greek'.

The woman soon returned, and before she could speak, I asked if I was dressed well enough. I excused myself by saying that I'd come straight from the kitchens.

'The guests aren't concerned about anything except drinking and talking about themselves,' she said and gave me a wink.

There was a long table of food and wine in the large hall where the guests were assembled. Alexander lay in a corner of the room, sleeping on a divan. I took a deep breath and went over to him, fixed my eyes on his face, took up the silver plate with its remnants of nuts and fruit, and carried it out into the kitchen. The women in there smiled, nodded but hardly had time to exchange a word. I looked around and asked the servers if they'd seen Aristotle. They told me that he'd gone back to Athens earlier in the day. A little later I asked if Priamos had been there. One shrugged her shoulders, the other said he'd been in attendance at the admiral's do, but when the king had become completely drunk, four soldiers had arrived and taken Priamos away.

'Who gave the order?'

'The regent.'

'You mean Antipater,' I said.

The youngest woman nodded.

At that moment I could have made an excuse and left the party. I stayed on. I wasn't myself. I was outside my own body.

I continued carrying plates and mugs in and out. The other women began rinsing. They wanted to get finished. Their legs were tired from running back and forth. Among the guests I came across someone I hadn't noticed before. Iollas. Fortunately he didn't recognize me. I'd met him in my early days at the palace. Very friendly with Medios, according to Alexander. Officially he was still the king's cup-bearer but neither Alexander nor Priamos trusted him now. That was why Alexander had given Priamos the responsibility of checking what he was served.

I never realized that Iollas was Cassander's brother and your son, Antipater, until I heard a conversation between the guests.

A few days before, Alexander had mentioned how angry you were with Olympias. For some years she'd been claiming that you wanted to overthrow her son. Alexander had said the claims were groundless. But when Alexander's informants in Athens reported your fury at the news that the king wished to make Babylon the capital of the realm, his tone changed. A month ago, Alexander asked you to leave Athens and come to Babylon. I heard from Alexander that you imagined you were going to be executed. Nevertheless you came. Presumably your men reported the state the king was in? Now he lay defenceless in the corner and slept, surrounded by his enemies.

I uttered Persian monosyllables and tried to seem indifferent to what you were talking or whispering about. Several times I felt for the nail to make sure it was in its proper place.

You drank less than the others, but made up for it by eating more. It wasn't hard to see that you had the measure of things and were the undisputed centre of attention. Admiral Nearchus was shorter than I remembered him, hunchbacked, with a face that shone round his blue nose. Twice, while the king lay in the corner and slept, I heard him say that Alexander was no longer capable of strategic military planning:

'You all know how tragic it was that Alexander involved Lydia in the war. A hopeless people. With an army no one deserves. And now the little that's left of it is lying outside the city walls, stinking.'

I almost dropped my tray. The admiral studied the people nodding around him.

'I said it would fail, don't you remember? Lydia's twenty thousand men were useless. The phalanx was reorganized against my will. Of the sixteen soldiers in each section only four were Macedonian, and of the other twelve, the majority were Lydians or Asians. You wouldn't listen to me then.'

Nearchus continued eagerly:

'The king has no notion of how to attack Arabia.'

The first time he said that, you and the others gave him a sceptical look, Antipater. The second time you cut him short:

'The idea of attacking is suicidal and senseless. I'll hear no more about it.'

There were nods from around the table. Nearchus tried to break in repeatedly, but was ignored.

'Let me tell you, Antipater—one of the best cures for arrogance is seasickness. When you're slumped over the rail, you soon forget your bad habits,' Nearchus shouted.

'A new front would be dangerous for everyone,' you replied.

'The Arabians will attack if we don't,' said Nearchus.

Medios turned to you, clearly interested in what was developing.

You shrugged your shoulders, turned and walked slowly over to the table with the fruit. Nearchus was furious and tried to run after you. Iollas hurried over to Nearchus and jabbed a finger in the admiral's chest.

'Sit.'

Nearchus stumbled backward, fell and found himself sitting bewildered on the floor.

Medios sat among the cushions in the light of the smoky lamp, the shadow of his head nodding on the wall as he listened to what was being said. Medios constantly put his hands to his temples, closed his eyes and moved his lips without producing any sound. He attempted to rise, then slipped back among the cushions, into a state of apparent tranquillity. He began to laugh without any obvious cause. No one tried to quieten him. After a while he said, 'Farewell, farewell', as if speaking to a mistress who mustn't be discovered through a crack in a door. It seemed as if Medios, bit by bit, was liberating himself from the rest of the company. He simply discarded the ties that bound him to the rest of you. It's possible that pain, sun or many years of wine-drinking had caused his face to look so swollen. When he started coughing, I took a step away from him.

Alexander was oblivious to all that was taking place around him.

The youngest man of the party kept close to you and Medios. He was probably about my age. I didn't know what he was called, until I was about to go home. His was a singular face, in which life had expunged all expression behind the light blonde moustache. He was elegantly attired in a deep red tunic, and appeared to be very fastidious.

Several times I had my back turned to you. I overheard the young man say:

'The silver tankard of strychnine is in the cupboard.'

'Speak more quietly, can't you,' you replied and walked away.

Nearchus might have recognized me if he hadn't been so drunk. I must have been mad. I saw no abyss, I didn't look down, I didn't look back, just straight ahead.

You quoted Aristotle's words about tyranny: 'No free man would endure such a regime.' The men nodded, several of them looked over at Alexander and smiled. Some cocked their heads. You clapped your hands:

'His brutality and drunkenness beget nothing but resistance,' you said, evidently confident that Alexander wasn't in a fit state to register a single word.

'In the past his cruelty could be a deterrent, something with which to terrify the enemy,' Iollas said. 'Now it's no longer effective, more and more people notice what an awful state he's in.'

Nearchus woke up, cleared his throat and said, after ascertaining that the king was still asleep:

'No one apart from his mother and the queen will mourn the tyrant.'

Even then, as I studied Alexander's ruddy, powerful face, with its deep folds, its full mouth with the characteristic lower lip, the still muscular body, I had to admit that I felt tenderness towards him. The revelation made me blush.

His breathing was irregular, it paused several times. I don't know whether that caused me anxiety or relief. People whispered that it would take too long for Alexander to drink himself to death. 'He's extremely tough,' I heard someone behind me murmur.

Nearchus had a genteel way of speaking, as if the sound came from some antiquated instrument, but despite this his words were intoned with a self-confidence that could make you feel inferior. Had I dared to say anything, I'd have had the sensation of slipping and falling.

Even when you people assume a phoney vulgarity, Antipater, you hold on to the self-assured tone with that whipcrack cadence, the one you use when talking to servants, like me.

I felt myself tensing several times, but there were also moments when I saw your dignity seeping away, like fat into an open fire.

You said in a kindly tone:

'Our ruler hasn't drunk anything for a while, isn't he happy in our company?'

Medios woke up, jumped to his feet, took the hint and shouted in Alexander's ear:

'Now we shall honour Heracles with a good, long toast.'

Alexander opened his eyes, stared at Medios and tried to rise, without succeeding. Sleep had clearly enabled him to drink once more. The men surrounding him clapped and cheered with each cup he emptied. Medios called:

'You have outshone your heroes, Alexander: Heracles, Dionysus and Achilles. None of them succeeded in becoming king of Macedonia, ruler of the Greek city states, a pharaoh and a god in Egypt, absolute ruler of Asia . . .'

'A toast to your future son! I suggest we drain the cups three times.'

Alexander nodded. His expression was grave. He made as if to say something, but then forgot what it was, and emptied his cup. You others pretended to drink, apart from Nearchus.

When Alexander seemed to be dozing off again, Medios nudged him.

'It's disappointing when you don't drink as much as Heracles used to.'

Dutifully, Alexander drank.

You sang a paean to the king and laughed when he closed his eyes and smiled back wanly at your praise. Am I right?

A dark patch between Alexander's legs slowly spread. Several people pointed. I felt embarrassment and grief before anger came. Was that the first time I noticed that his face was different? It had assumed a leaden hue, his eyes were empty and his cheekbones even more prominent.

Iollas leant towards you, Antipater, and asked something I couldn't catch, apart from the word 'kitchen'. You shook your head.

'It'll sort itself out,' you said.

You hoped Alexander would drink himself to death. Don't deny it. Remember what you did next? You turned to the assembly and cried:

'Our ruler, our own god, you will soon eclipse Heracles himself in the field of drinking, too. A pity Dionysus couldn't be among us tonight. Cheers!'

Suddenly Alexander opened his eyes and looked straight at me.

'Penelope, so you're here,' he said loudly.

I pretended not to see or hear him. A short while later he fell asleep again. Those closest to him shook their heads and went on talking. I could breathe again. What was the worst that could happen to me? A knife, a sword, a spear in the heart? At least I would be spared a long and agonizing death. Now everybody, including me, could see his wretchedness. It was then, at that moment, the true realization came, that Alexander was unable to protect me any longer.

I backed into the kitchen. Priamos had taught me that strychnine is a clear, bitter liquid. I began to search for the tankard. It was easy to find. It had been placed behind some cooking pots. Unobserved, I managed to pour some of its contents into a wine cup and left the kitchen.

Now it was time to put an end to the humiliation. He didn't deserve it. I glanced quickly in his direction. I thought of my lover, once so virile, the ruler who gave orders that everyone obeyed. Once, I'd trembled with desire at the sight of him, there'd been a thudding in my ears, my mouth had been dry, my throat constricted, it had been unendurable, it had been delightful. How I'd admired him. Now all I felt was despair, distaste, pain. And concern.

I placed the cup directly in front of him and walked back towards the kitchen. I turned and saw that he was about to fall asleep. I didn't know what to do. I walked back to Alexander and, as if by accident, knocked against his foot.

Another song of praise was sung. During the applause Alexander took the cup and downed the contents in one draught. Priamos had taught me that wine disguises strychnine's bitterness. Alexander began shouting unintelligibly.

You nodded to the pair of soldiers by the door. They ran up, took hold of the king and lugged him out. Alexander didn't open his eyes. Now he's dead, I thought.

The party broke up. The guests hurried home. The king was laid on a handcart at the back of the house and pushed home by the two soldiers. I ran out on to the steps, I wanted to see him one last time. But he'd disappeared.

Medios came into the kitchen, fetched the silver tankard and told us to go home. He shouted for you, Antipater. His eyes were red. I picked up his comment, 'But we have no guarantee that things will be better now.' As he went up the stairs to the first floor, I noticed he was gazing down into the tankard. The tired old man gave a groan those who remained couldn't fail to notice.

The youth with the moustache offered to accompany me part of the way. He introduced himself as Ephippus. He was the only man who seemed to be sober. I shook my head and pretended I didn't understand what he was saying. He exchanged a few words with you, which I didn't catch. What I saw, was your shrug of the shoulders.

I look at the name again: Ephippus, I repeat the syllables, murmur the name several times. I'm sure I've heard it before. At last I work out where I know it from. Ephippus wrote an eyewitness account of Alexander's final months. We have no idea who employed him,

and he says nothing at all about that particular night. But he gave a comprehensive account of the king's drinking habits. One of Ephippus' comments has stuck in my mind, 'Alexander was a thoroughly violent man with no respect for human life.'

I walked alone, it was getting light. The wind from across the hills, was colder than usual. I could hear a cock crow, as if I were walking in some peaceful spot, indeed, peace in Babylon might seem the norm and the wind that muffled the cock-crow, the most dramatic event in the city that morning. Soon the stalls on the side streets would open. I shop at several of them for Priamos, for goods that aren't sold in the market-place. People were already sweeping the streets, they said we should give thanks for yesterday's rain, pointing out that heat-waves make it difficult to speak because the words begin to burn in the mouth, they shrivel on the tongue, until there isn't a peep left in us.

In the distance, blue shadows fell from the mountains. Just in front of me on the sandy road, a yellow lizard poked its head out of a hole, and as soon as it felt the sun, it darted off and hid in the shade of a stone.

I walked in the direction of a man who stood down by the river fishing. He glanced up at me for a moment then, using a long stick, he manoeuvred two grey planks in to the bank. I stared down at the water, between the flowering cypresses on the riverside. The water rocked almost calmly above the current, which slipped and twisted about itself. The sun caused the shadows to caress a pair of thrushes which were probing the damp soil with their beaks.

As I passed the fisherman, I noticed how thin he was. His beard and hair were grey and sparse. I was so close that I could look into his eyes. He didn't like this and turned away. He stooped and drank some of the cloudy water.

A grey, barely visible mist seeped out of the earth and rose towards the treetops. Far away, the hillsides were still in shadow. A few swallows zigzagged to and fro high in the air. One of them dived towards a puddle, caught something in its beak and skimmed the water with its tail feathers before mounting up high and disappearing with the others just as the sun came out in a blaze.

Just imagine if I'd possessed a little of the calm of Alexander's old friend, the Indian Brahmin Kalanos. Alexander described him as an ideal, a man who didn't allow himself to be ruled by the fear of pain. For two years he was a member of the king's retinue. For most of that time he'd been ill. According to Kalanos, an evil fire was consuming everything within him. He rarely referred to the pain that wracked his body. Alexander said that when he looked into his face, he could discern small wrinkles that betrayed his agonies. At Persepolis he made up his mind to die. Alexander tried to talk the Brahmin out of it, but he was unshakeable. He said he yearned for home. Kalanos said he wanted to be like the roses that whither and eventually return to the soil.

Alexander liked him. He told him so. The Brahmin thanked and said that if that was the case, he wanted the king to begin making a pyre. Alexander believed that he had to grant the wish.

Kalanos put on his finest white tunic, with gold bands at the neck and sleeves, and rode out to the pyre. As he dismounted from his horse, he said:

'I've never felt such a longing before.'

He offered up a prayer, sprinkled himself with holy water and cut off a lock of his long, grey hair to give to Alexander as a keepsake. That done he enjoined Alexander and his men not to grieve:

'The best way you can honour my memory, is to drink yourselves into oblivion.'

'Don't you want something to lessen the pain?' Alexander asked.

Kalanos calmly shook his head. Before Alexander could say another word, Kalanos gave his servants orders to light the kindling. The guru pushed aside some dry trunks and planks and entered the pyre.

When Alexander told me about him, he closed his eyes and grimaced as if he was practising enduring pain.

I followed the path that ended close to the royal wing of the palace. Lysimachus and Roxane might be at the king's side. I realized that I couldn't make it to my own room before the start of my morning's work. This part of the palace was completely silent. My lame foot ached.

I crept up the back stairs to the king's apartments.

The door was open. In semi-darkness I carefully climbed the stairs to the king's room. I halted in front of the bed chamber and listened. Cautiously, I pushed open the heavy door.

Luckily, no one was there. I hastened into the library. On the table lay several letters from the king's mother. Had someone been in here recently? On one open scroll were the words, 'Dear Son, Pausanias must be dealt with as quickly as possible after the murder. His mind is unstable. He's so desperate and unhappy that he could reveal his taskmasters. Pausanias is the ideal murderer, but not fit to live. The first thrust must come with a force that only six months' hate and unrequited love can muster.'

I had little time, even so when I noticed a scroll from Aristotle I couldn't resist it. It was still quiet outside.

Aristotle addressed Alexander like a child, instead of being grateful for all the objects, the careful reports and sketches he'd sent him. What impressive copies Alexander possessed. He also had a large collection of erotic art from Egypt and India. There were details of the preparations for the battles of Granicus, Issus, Gaugamela and Hydaspes. I didn't manage to open the scrolls on the sieges of Tyre and Gaza. Dreams and unsent correspondence were exciting, but my greatest surprise was reserved for the scrolls entitled 'Encounters with Nearchus'. Here he'd drawn and written about creatures I've never heard of: mackerel sharks and dolphin monkeys. I saw drawings and descriptions of pyramid lizards, giraffe cactuses and the moon creature that lives entirely off moonlight. The creature resembled a huge quadruped with a shell-like a shield on its back, and a mace for a tail.

I also found my own letters to Alexander. The ones I'd tried to forget. The ones I'd written, giddy with love. I forced myself to read, 'I will be your most dutiful army, for ever.' I took the letters and wanted to burn them. I wanted to turn them all to ashes, to make them part of the invisible library, where our love belongs. Several times I tried to strike the flints to make fire but I was too nervous. It took too long. I heard heavy footsteps on the stairs, I dropped the flints and ran in the opposite direction, and made my escape, unobserved, down the corridor to the kitchens.

Priamos should have been working that day, too. His second-in-command, Heron, whom I'd never seen before because he worked the opposite shifts, came running to say that Alexander had survived an assassination attempt which showed, yet gain, that our ruler was protected by the gods.

'Sadly, Priamos was a traitor. People tell me you did whatever you liked when he was around. What did he get in return? Did you go to bed with him?'

I felt dizzy, I grasped the nearest table top and said it was a joy and a relief to hear that things had gone well with the king. Heron nodded. He was one of those types who like passing on bad news, and dwelling on pain, suffering and macabre sights. No sooner had he finished telling me, than he saw someone else he could tell the story to, with even greater exaggeration and zest. Once he was out of sight, I got out the nail, washed it quickly and replaced it in its drawer.

I was silent for the rest of the working day. I was cleaning whitefish. Cutting off the head, sticking my knife in the belly, peeling back the greyish-white flesh and removing the guts, rinsing the fish in a basin of water and then throwing the fillets in a heap on the stone slab. I kept raising my head and looking at the door. It couldn't be long before the bodyguards came and asked me questions and then executed me. I mustn't, at any cost, mention Priamos' name.

They didn't come. In the ensuing days I worked for as long as I could, even though it was unbearably hot. When I wasn't preparing fowls, fish or mushrooms, or shopping for Heron, I lay in my room in bed. I said little or nothing to the others, but thought all the more about Alexander, going round and round, in labyrinths I couldn't escape from.

Recently, whenever Zara has brought me something to eat, she's been very unwilling to talk about the king.

There's no harm in her. She's basically loyal to any ruler. When she mentions the king, her eyes open wide. According to Zara, Alexander has suffered a high fever in recent days. He's constantly being placed in cooling baths, but the fever won't leave him. He spends the night in the bathhouse at the palace. In the morning he's carried back to the audience chamber. Late in the evenings the servants attempt to feed him, making sacrifices to the gods at the same time.

I blame myself for killing an innocent servant, but the greatest self-reproach I feel is for not getting enough strychnine into Alexander, so that he'd be spared these days.

'The king has given his signet ring to Antipater's man, General Perdiccas, you know,' Zara said.

'Why did he get it?' I asked.

'Antipater asked the king who should assume power. He said, 'The strongest', and pointed to Perdiccas.'

'So Alexander can talk?'

She looked at me in confusion.

'Has someone told you all this?' I asked.

She turned and left without answering my question.

Now, as the end is drawing close, I've changed my mind. I want to live after Alexander's death. I've developed the self-centred notion that I don't deserve to die; not just that, but I believe I deserve it less than him, the king.

Outside, in the square, crowds are constantly arriving from all parts of the kingdom. They want confirmation that Alexander is still alive, that he's still able to lead them and be their father and protector. I want to live so that I can tell them that they no longer have a protecting hand over them, they have no support, no succour.

Now the gods are being invoked as well.

Soon there'll be nothing else to call on.

Delicate shafts of reddish light strike through the hole in the wall, enough to outline the few objects within this small room, but too little for the eyes to make out the far corner, where the oil lamp's tiny flame is about to expire. Most people who aren't at war, die in their beds at night, as they squeeze the hand of someone who's dear to them. That's an experience I shall never know.

I woke up grinding my teeth. My jaw was clamped shut. It felt as if my teeth were going to break. By massaging my jaw muscles I managed to get my mouth open. Outside, it was becoming light. There was still a little time before I was due down in the kitchens. Were they watching me to see if I was in league with others? I got ready quickly and dressed. Outside it was misty with some low dots of cloud, the way it often is before a really hot day. I wanted to go down and look at the Euphrates, where the bridge crosses it.

I caught sight of a young couple by the river bank. They lay closely wrapped in each other. I thought of the first stroll Alexander and I had taken along the bank. Alexander carried a shoulder bag and a straw hat. He clutched the shoulder bag so tightly, it might have been his own fate he was guarding. When I asked what was in it, he wouldn't answer. To my surprise, he took my hand and walked through the reeds down to the water's edge, removed the bag from his shoulder, opened it and pulled out a collapsible fishing-rod, just like the one we have in the kitchens. Priamos had given it to Alexander. He asked if I wanted to fish first, I shook my head. A man came towards us up the path. He was walking a quadruped so thin it looked as if it had swallowed a cage in order to resemble a horse. Its head drooped. Its eyes were large and lustreless. The man shouted that there weren't any fish just there. We must go further upstream. Alexander shrugged his shoulders. He'd only get a few small fish at best, and he was much more interested in describing dolphins, sharks and more particularly whales, starfish, and squid so huge that they could consume the largest sailing ships in existence.

On that first visit to the river bank I hadn't realized it was Admiral Nearchus who'd fed him these tales.

It wouldn't be long before the sun penetrated the mist and the heat crept up and woke the couple. It would be the worst tribulation of their day. The water chuckled close by them, but only loudly enough to lull. They hadn't yet realized that time was precious. They were still revelling in it, careless that later in life they would reproach themselves for their folly. Once, I'd been so shortsighted that I hoped my youth would leave me, I'd longed to see it vanish.

Alexander dies. Plutarch hasn't been born. The plans to attack Arabia and Scythia are dropped, as is the idea of conquering the coast around the western Mediterranean. The Macedonian generals who'd been at Medios' party, begin to jostle for power. The Greek city states declare independence. The rebellion is stamped out. Antipater punishes Athens by suspending democracy and banishing a large part of its population. The Athenian leader, Demosthenes, commits suicide. The realm is split into three.

Alexander's son by Roxane, Alexander IV, rules from birth, jointly with Alexander's mentally retarded brother, Philip III. Roxane executes Alexander's two other wives, Stateira II and Parysatis II. Antipater's son, Cassander, kills Roxane and Alexander IV. Philip III and his wife, Eurydice, are killed by Olympias. Olympias is killed by Cassander. Subsequently, Barsine and Alexander's firstborn son, Heracles, are murdered at the hands of unidentified killers. 'This is the end,' Jim Morrison sings in 1967.

The people responsible for Alexander's death, had the best of intentions, but a well-intentioned deed often leads to unintended consequences:

A friend, a believer, pushed me and my wheelchair out into the holy water at Lourdes to cure my paralysis. I'm an atheist. He was concerned for my welfare. I didn't want to disappoint him. I wanted to console him for having to see me in this condition. When I came out again, I hadn't altered, but the right wheel of my chair was wrecked. Then the left one hit a stone. I fell out and ended up lying on my back. All I know is that the body is nature's portion, a certainty I'm reminded of more and more frequently. I have written with my hand's five fingers, thirty-five muscles, the two thousand nerve cells in each of my fingertips. I write on the road to death, before I turn to dust, earth, steam, clouds. Like Phyllis, I have little time. I write because I must.

❧

The wind blew through the big deciduous trees, with gentle breath. The first rays of sun brought a warmth one could only just feel. Above me stretched a blue geography of clouds and shifting continents. Between two glints of sun my shady meditations grew, even though I concentrated on the ever-changing cloud formations. I didn't succeed for long. At my feet I glimpsed a caterpillar. I crouched down. It was blind and lumpish, but capable of spinning a thread that would make a cocoon. Within it, tiny creatures with white wings would develop. These are the only angels I've seen.

'That's her,' Heron shouted eagerly.

He came running up with five soldiers.

The couple woke up and screamed, and then realized it wasn't them, but me the men were after. I just stood there. Heron told the soldiers, as they tied my hands behind my back, that I was the one who knew the king.

His face was red with excitement and he repeated several times that it was me.

When I'd been trussed, he tried to kick me, but the eldest of the soldiers managed to stop him. The youngest asked:

'You work in the kitchens at the palace?'

'Yes,' replied the zealous Heron.

'Keep quiet, she'll do the answering,' shouted the soldier.

I nodded.

It was neither the time nor the place to make my confession. I can't speak Babylonian. Meaning is often botched in translation, and sometimes lost altogether. The gulf between Babylonian and Greek is great, as great as the gulf between sun and moon. It's like that whispering game, where a sentence is broken down word by word, changing from one person to the next, until it ends up as a travesty of the once so carefully crafted line.

For a moment I thought of begging for my life. I dismissed the idea.

The soldiers pushed me along in front of them. A butterfly rose into the sky in front of me, red and black.

I could have chosen to keep silent, I chose what I believed would give me dignity: to write what the majority want us to forget. Our dignity and our thoughts are probably the only things we control ourselves, regardless of sex or rank.

I am complicit in much of what Alexander has done, I was his ally and could have altered some of his decisions. I make no excuses. What gives me pause for thought, is how self-engrossed I was when I killed that young servant on the way to Medios' house. I killed him so that he wouldn't prevent me from seeing Alexander and humbling him one more time. My thirst for revenge was boundless.

If I'd been able to explain why I loved him, I might have been able to extricate myself. If I'd been able to account for it, I'd have found the words to describe it. I don't understand it. What I do know is that I am Phyllis, whom many in the future will label a prostitute. I was Alexander's lover, one who will depart this life with so many questions, on her way up to the sky, or into the blue abyss, the kingdom of the dolphins, into the sea, the earth or the gentle horizon.

There was a shout outside. I looked through the hole. A noisy crowd. The guards didn't stand in their way. Ordinary people, no soldiers. They were shouting my name. They were clutching stones. Some of them yelled that that they wanted to come and get me. At last, Alexander and I will be free of the people, live like air among them, like memories. We shall forego future dusks in Babylon. No one will see us again in the evenings, as the blue night falls across the world.

They forced their way into my room. They didn't touch what I was writing. They dragged me out, they threw stones at me. Women, men and children were all throwing. They didn't know me. They'd never seen me before. They screamed that I was getting my just deserts, and that the king was dead.

I hadn't imagined it happening like this.

The first stones struck my arms, hips and legs. One hit my neck. They were aiming for my head, but missed. The commandant shouted that it was dark now, and that they'd have to come back when it grew light.

TWENTY-ONE NOTES

I have allowed myself to update Phyllis' text to our own time and render it in my own voice. The fact that she is a woman, a cook, and in some people's eyes a prostitute or a fiction, isn't sufficient to dismiss what has been written.

✻

The revelation in the letter that women were part of the campaign, may come as a surprise to some. There are many indications, as in countless other armies, that women formed part of the rearguard as spouses, prostitutes, cooks, servers, washerwomen, latrine emptiers, musicians and seamstresses. Disease and death also conceivably forced women to assume other roles that we know nothing about. What makes the letter so interesting is that the role of women in the campaign isn't cited in contemporary sources about Alexander and his army. But the fact that they went unrecorded, doesn't mean they didn't make a contribution. What we do know is that Aristotle, Callisthenes the king's official historian, and Plutarch, too, provided few or no descriptions of women. Plato, by contrast, did. Even though women went largely unnoticed at that period, a few are mentioned: Olympias, Alexander's mother, is constantly referred to as a loving parent but also as a power politician. His wet nurse Lanike came from a noble family and meant much to Alexander. She was also described by Arrian and Curtius, for example. Nor had Alexander any qualms about listening to advice from the priestess at Delphi (Plutarch).

Timocleia was the widow of a general from Thebes, a city Alexander and his army had crushed. She was charged with the murder of a Thracian officer. She killed him by pushing him down a well after he'd raped her. Alexander reprieved both Timocleia and her children, because he thought she was brave (Plutarch).

When the army took Halicarnassus, present-day Bodrum, Pixodarus became ruler after unjustly seizing the throne from Queen Ada. Alexander reinstated her, and kept in touch with her for the remainder of his life (Arrian, Diodorus).

After the Battle of Issus, the Persian king, Darius III, managed to escape. Alexander took Darius' mother, Sisygambis, and his wife, Stateira, prisoner together with their ladies-in-waiting. A female orchestra consisting of 329 musicians was also captured. As if that wasn't enough, considerable numbers of Persian army wives and children were taken, including Barsine, with whom Alexander had a son, Heracles (Curtius, Justin). He forbade his soldiers to sexually exploit the thousands of women taken.

One of the hardest chapters in the army's history was the march across the Gedrosian desert, which caused unimaginable suffering and losses. Ancient historians wondered why he chose to cross the desert, particularly with so many women and children in tow (Arrian, Curtius, Diodorus).

✳

All that survives is a transcript of Phyllis' letter. The scroll on which it was originally written is missing. Nothing in the letter contradicts other known sources from Alexander's time.

There are many motifs of Phyllis sitting on Aristotle. The most famous is by Hans Holbein the Younger from Basle (1522). Phyllis Riding Aristotle is a bronze sculpture from Holland (c.1400). The artist is unknown. The sculpture is in the Metropolitan Museum. The motif is also found on an ivory box which was made in Paris (c.1330–50), now in Walters Art Gallery.

✳

Phyllis isn't mentioned in Queen Roxane's surviving scrolls. After Roxane's death they were appropriated by Regent Antipater. The scrolls were rediscovered in Constantinople in 694 CE according to a number of sources. These are unreliable, in common with most of the others I'm acquainted with. Some believe the scrolls were lost during the Crusaders' attack and sacking of the Byzantine Empire's capital in 1204. The scrolls had the following catalogue headings:

ΠΣ	IB
ΠΣ	IIA
Π	IB
ΠΣΥΩ	ΔΑ
ΣΩΥ	ΔΔΠΙ

ΥΣ	IIII
ΩΠΣ	III
ΩΠΣΑΒ	I
Υ	II
Π	III
ΥΠΩΣΒ	ΠΠII
ΥΠΩΑ	ΔΔI

*

Historians today often assess sources, be they writings or artefacts like coins, weapons and clothes, against four criteria: whether the source is genuine or false; whether it's recent or distant in time; whether the source is influenced by other sources. And, as an extension of the last criterion: whether the source is biased. It's easy to overlook the fact that a source can lie or be wrong, even though all the above criteria have been met.

No documents in Alexander's own hand have been preserved, but some letters attributed to him may be genuine. The administrator, Eumenes of Cardia, kept logbooks, *Ephemerides*, detailing the king's daily doings during Alexander's final years. But these describe very little of a political or military nature, unlike the letter from Phyllis.

Another eyewitness from Alexander's time is Ephippus, the man Phyllis met that fateful evening at Medios' house. He is cited by Athenaeus, among others.

Callisthenes took part in many of the campaigns until he was executed in 327 BCE, as Phyllis describes in her letter.

Callisthenes filled the roles of historian, propagandist and war correspondent. His work *Deeds of Alexander* (328 BCE) describes the first part of Alexander's reign. In addition to Callisthenes, Ptolemy, a general and later king of Egypt, provides first-hand accounts of various battles. These endeavour to place the author in a favourable light. Aristobulus, a Greek engineer on Alexander's staff, and Onesicritus, the captain of the king's personal vessel, provide detailed accounts. And Admiral Nearchus described several naval expeditions. Unfortunately, all the primary source material has been lost. There is a great deal of secondary source material based on several of the missing scrolls, which are referred to and quoted from.

The oldest is Diodorus, the Greek historian who based his description on Cleitarchus, who was probably present in Babylon when Alexander died. The Roman Curtius wrote his work *Historiae Alexandri Magni Macedonis* in 40 CE. There is some consensus that the author was especially interested in anecdotal and sensational material about Alexander.

Plutarch, a Greek, wrote about Alexander between 110 and 115 CE. These texts are often referred to as his moral writings and his biographies. The latter appear late on in his work. They are entitled *Bioi Paralleloi* (Parallel Lives), because in each he compares a Greek to a Roman. Alexander and Caesar form such a pair. Plutarch's highly favourable depiction of Alexander greatly influenced people such as William Shakespeare, Johann Wolfgang von Goethe and Napoleon Bonaparte.

Another Greek, Arrian, produced his work about 120 CE. He maintained he was trying to avoid biased opinions, and he named his sources. To distinguish truth from fiction, he compared the general veracity of his sources and weighed them against one another. If that was impossible, he presented more than one version of events and let the reader decide.

Justin (Marcus Junianus Justinius), a Roman who lived at the beginning of the fourth century CE, is most widely known for his shortened version of Pompeius Trogus' *Historiae Philippicae*, which in turn was based on Cleitarchus' description.

The works of the historians mentioned above form the basis for the picture of Alexander and his age, as conveyed by modern historians and writers. They have their own styles, their own favourites, their own narrative.

A work that has almost certainly influenced more than a few historians, is the one known as the *Alexander Romance*. It was written around 200 BCE. The author is unknown. In the Middle Ages when there was much interest in Alexander, the author was thought to be Callisthenes, but contemporary historians regard this as unlikely. The author has been somewhat unflatteringly dubbed 'pseudo-Callisthenes'. But the book has survived the centuries. It was translated into Latin in 300 CE, and from 960 CE it was recreated in other European, African and Asiatic languages. The work is an epic narrative and omits the final months in Babylon.

*

Homer's extraordinary story about Troy has been told for more than two and a half millennia: The Greeks had besieged the city for over ten years, before suddenly disappearing one night, much to the Trojans' surprise. Only an enormous wooden construction shaped like a horse remained before the city gate, together with a Greek called Sinon. He had been condemned by his fellow countrymen to be left to die at the hands of their enemies. The Greeks left the tree horse standing outside the gate. The Trojans called for the horse to be hauled into the city, to serve as a memorial to the Trojan victory over the Greeks. Cassandra shouted, 'Don't move the monster inside the walls.' According to Homer, she was supposed to have implored the men to see sense. Cassandra was certain they were the victims of a Greek stratagem. She despaired at her own people's refusal to listen to her. Phyllis believed that Odysseus won, not on account of any bravery or wisdom but—somewhat ingloriously—because of the Trojans' own stupidity. 'Cassandra's anxiety displayed no more brilliance or clairvoyance than might have been expected from any reasonably endowed person, according to Phyllis. Odysseus' 'stratagem' was at best foolhardy. The Trojans pulled the huge horse through the city gate. As soon as it had been manoeuvred into place, they began to celebrate.

Sinon remained sober. Just before sunrise, he released the soldiers inside the horse, and opened the city gate allowing the Greek forces into Troy. The question, which is probably better left unasked, is how fifty men could stand inside the horse for twenty-four hours, and how even after that they were in a condition to fight.

*

Pella in Macedonia, where both Alexander and Phyllis grew up, was destroyed in 168 BCE. Twenty-two years later, the area was turned into a Roman province. The city was founded in 399 BCE, by King Archelaus of Macedonia. Pella was the capital when Alexander and his father, Philip II, reigned.

*

Babylon was an Akkadian city state established in 1867 BCE in ancient Mesopotamia. The remains of the city can be found in the modern province of Babil in Iraq, fifty miles south of Baghdad. Babylon was the capital of the Neo-Babylonian Empire, which in 550 BCE covered half of Egypt, half of Saudi Arabia, Palestine, Israel, Jordan, Syria, a large part of Anatolia and Iraq. The city was built on both banks of the Euphrates. Several of the best-known edifices were built below Nebuchadnezzar II's palace. Phyllis refers to some, such as the Hanging Gardens and the Tower of Babel—a three hundred-foot-high step pyramid, which is also described in the Book of Genesis. It's worth noting that the enormous height and size of the structure made a terrifying impression on many of Phyllis' contemporaries. In the Bible it was seen as an example of man's arrogant attitude towards God.

In 331 BCE, the Persian emperor, Darius III, was defeated by Alexander the Great at the battle of Gaugamela, and Babylon fell under Alexander's control.

✻

The name Alexander means 'protector of men'. Derived from the Greek *Alexandros*, which in turn is formed from the constituents *alex* and *andros*. 'Alex' comes from the Greek verb 'alexein', which means to defend or help, while *andros* is the genitive form of the Greek word 'aner', which means man.

✻

Bucephalus was the name of Alexander's principal steed. Some believe that Bucephalus, like all Thessalian horses, bore a brand in the shape of a bull's head. Other sources maintain that branding wasn't common until after Bucephalus' time. The latter camp believes that Alexander's horse got its name because its head was as large and broad as a bull's. Bucephalus was killed at the battle of Hydaspes, fought against the Indian king, Porus, in 326 BCE. Bucephalus is regarded as the world's most famous horse. The city of Bucephala was named after him.

✻

Alexander the Great is a title he never used himself. The honorific first gained currency among the Roman aristocracy, about a century after Alexander's death.

✻

Phyllis is always referring to wine and alcohol in her meetings with Alexander. A number of present-day historians point to the same thing. Robin Lane Fox's *Alexander the Great* (1973) mentions, for example, that in the final month of his life alone, Alexander indulged in three heavy binges which each required thirty-six hours' sleep to recover from. This doesn't include the fourth and final bout, which Phyllis describes in the last part of her narrative. The Greeks drank watered-down wine. Most Macedonians drank it undiluted. Alexander and Philip II were no exception. This was one of the main reasons for the Greeks' frequent reference to the Macedonians as barbarians. Aelian in *Varia Historia* noted that in October the pattern of alcohol intake was as follows, 'On the fifth day of the month Alexander drank with Evenaios. On the sixth he slept as a result of his drinking, awaking only to discuss the next day's march with his generals, and to decide that they should make an early start. On the seventh and eighth days he slept'. Aelian suggests this was the cycle he followed throughout the final year of his life.

*

One theory is that Alexander fell victim to malaria. A few weeks before he died he journeyed to the malaria-infested delta of the Euphrates. Other doctors have suggested that the malaria developed into leukaemia, and that it was this that killed him (Fritz Schachermeyer in *Aleksander in Babylon und die Reichsordnung nach seinen Toden*, 1970). Some believe that his demise was the result of a serious nervous disorder caused by an aggressive salmonella bacterium (David W. Oldach et al., 'A Mysterious Death' in *The New England Journal of Medicine*, 1998).

However, all ancient sources point to poison, especially strychnine, as the most likely cause of death. It's worth noting that Aristotle's student Theophrastus, in his work *Historia Plantarum*, says that strychnine's bitter taste should be masked by wine to get the victim to drink it more readily, as Phyllis describes in her letter.

Plutarch describes strychnine thus, 'The poison is said to be an icy liquid that drips like fine dew from a mountain near Nonacris. It is gathered up and stored in an ass' hoof, the only container that will hold it. Every other material is eaten away because it is so cold and bitter' (Plutarch, *Alexander and Cæsar*).

✳

According to Plutarch, the Athenian politician Demades found it impossible to believe the news of the king's demise, 'Alexander dead? Impossible. The whole world would have smelt the stench of his corpse.'

✳

Alexander died on 10 June 323 BCE, and was born on 20 July 356 BCE. Phyllis was born in Pella the same year. Phyllis uses no dates. Key ones linked to the episodes she describes are:

336 BCE Philip II is murdered and Alexander succeeds him as king.

331 BCE The city of Alexandria is founded in Egypt; the Persians are conquered after the battle of Gaugamela; Babylon and Susa are taken.

329 BCE Alexander's army crosses the Hindu Kush and occupies Bactria.

327 BCE Alexander marries Roxane; his army attacks India.

324 BCE Hephaestion dies; Alexander and Phyllis meet.

323 BCE Historical evidence indicates that Phyllis dies in June.

*

A few days after Alexander's death, expert Egyptian and Babylonian embalmers began to work on the king's corpse. General Perdiccas' plan was to have Alexander taken to Aigai, the traditional resting place of Macedonian rulers. Alexander was transported in a large and very beautiful hearse, drawn by sixty-four mules decked out in golden bells and crowns. His earthly remains lay beneath its roof in a golden coffin filled with aromatic herbs which had the added benefit of retarding the corpse's putrefaction. Ionian columns reminiscent of his childhood's Pella formed the sides of the hearse together with sculptures and paintings depicting his major battles. According to Diodorus, it took nearly two years to construct this temple on wheels.

Several decades later, Ptolemy II, moved the sarcophagus to Alexandria. Here a huge funerary monument was built enclosed by walls, called 'Sema' or 'Soma', which in Greek mean funerary monument and body respectively. A number of rulers visited the grave, including the Roman emperor Octavian, who took the name Augustus. When he went to kiss Alexander, he was mortified to find he'd broken the deceased's nose.

Alexander could be viewed inside a translucent coffin, probably made of alabaster. It was King Ptolemy X who'd had this sarcophagus fashioned out of a glass-like material. The Roman emperor Septimus Severus (193–211 CE) closed the gravesite for security reasons due to the crowds of tourists who wanted to see the coffin.

When Napoleon invaded Egypt in 1798, he gave orders for the coffin to be removed to Paris. The Corsican wished to be buried next to his hero. On the voyage to France, the ship carrying the coffin was captured by the British. In 1805, the British scholar Edward Clarke wrote *The Tomb of Alexander: A Dissertation of the Sarcophagus Brought from Alexandria and Now in the British Museum*. Clarke demonstrated that the sarcophagus wasn't that of Alexander, but the Egyptian Pharaoh Nectanebo II.

Since then, Alexander's grave has reportedly been located in Saida in Lebanon; Siwa in Egypt; Uzbekistan; Pakistan; in a cave in Illinois, USA; in St Marks, Venice; and in 2014 in Amphipolis.

✷

Roxane and Alexander's son was born in August 323 BCE. He was given the name Alexander IV. Little Alexander ruled jointly with Alexander's brother, the mentally retarded Philip III. Antipater's son, Cassander, killed both Roxane and Alexander IV in 310 (Diodorus, Justin and Pausanias.) Philip III and his wife Eurydice were murdered on the orders of Olympias in 317. In 315, Olympias was liquidated on the orders of Cassander, who controlled Macedonia. Shortly after Alexander died, his two other wives, Stateira II of Persia and Parysatis II of Persia, were both murdered by Queen Roxane (Plutarch). Alexander's first son, Heracles, was assassinated in 309 together with his mother Barsine (Diodorus, Justin and Plutarch).

*

There is a biblical reference to Alexander in the Book of Daniel. The prophet's visions concerning him are sombre: 'After this I saw in the night visions, and behold a fourth beast, dreadful and terrible, and strong exceedingly; and it had great iron teeth: it devoured and brake in pieces, and stamped in the residue with the feet of it: and it was diverse from all the beasts that there were before it; and it had ten horns.' Also the first book of Maccabees in the Apocrypha describes how Alexander plundered nation after nation and gradually became arrogant and 'evils were multiplied in the earth'. In later Jewish tradition the image of Alexander becomes more positive. The Judaeo-Greek historian Flavius Josephus portrays him as a good and god-fearing king in *Antiquitates Judaicae* (93–4 CE). A similar assessment can be found in the

Talmud, in a description of how Alexander threw himself to the ground before the high priests in the temple in Jerusalem, and in the story of how he was led by the God of Israel in his war with the Persians. Even the Koran mentions Alexander. The reference is very similar to the description in the Book of Daniel. He is called Zul-Karnayn, 'the two-horned one', a pious ruler who builds a wall in the Caucasus, as a bastion against the wicked races of Gog and Magog. In some Persian traditions, particularly the Zoroastrian, Alexander was regarded as evil personified. He was blamed for the burning of their sacred writings, the *Avesta*, when he set fire to the city of Persepolis.

*

According to Diodorus, certain individuals began to wear straw hats after Alexander's death, just as he had done, including the Macedonian generals Ptolemy, Seleucus and Perdiccas. It was important for the generals to show affinity and that they'd been part of the circle around their hero, as this was an advantage in getting the jobs they craved.

*

Sappho, whom Phyllis quotes from memory, lived on the island of Lesbos in the seventh century BCE. She was famous in her own time and has remained so. Sappho wrote in the first person and literary historians view her as pioneering the meticulous description of the individual's experience of love and loss:

> The silver moon is set;
> The Pleiades are gone;
> Half the long night is spent, and yet
> I lie alone.

Aristotle's teacher, Plato, declared:

> 'Some say the muses are nine in number; how careless!
> See, here is Sappho too, from Lesbos, the tenth.'

*

The name Phyllis is Greek and is derived from the word 'phullon' meaning 'leaf' (and 'foliage'). According to Greek tradition, Phyllis was reunited with her lover after her death. Then the leaves and the flowers budded on the almond tree.

Acknowledgements

My thanks to Kari Joynt, Geir Gulliksen, Ingeri Engelstad, Christine Amadou, Vigdis Hjorth, Jon Vidar Sigurdsson, Nora Skaug, Peter Normann Waage, Aristotle, Peter Green, N.G.L. Hammond, Frank L. Holt, Robin Lane Fox, Bengt Liljegren, Plutarch, Sappho, W. W. Tarn, Ian Worthington and others.

Translations of Sappho by J. H. Merivale and John Myers O'Hara.